FALLING FOR A HOOD KING 4

SHVONNE LATRICE

ABOUT THE AUTHOR

Other Works by Me:

Good Girls Love Thugs 1-5
Falling for a Hood King 1-4
Married to a Distinguished Thug 1-3
She's Gotta Have It 1-2
Me & My Dope Boy 1-3
Yazir & Nina 1-3
Forbidden Love with a Thug 1-3
You Needed Me 1-3
Shorty is in Love with a Real One 1-4
I Got Your Back 1-2
My Baby Is a West Coast King 1-4
Our Love Is the Realest 1-3
She Got It Bad for a Heartless Gangsta 1-4
She Got It Bad for a Heartless Gangsta: An AK Christmas
Hood Boyz Fall In Love Too 1-3
Nobody Can Love You Like Them Roughnecks Do 1-4
She Gave Her All to the Hood's Finest 1-5

Visit www.theshvonnelatrice.com for paperbacks!

facebook.com/ShvonneLatrice
twitter.com/siobhannoir
instagram.com/siobhannoir

Copyright © 2020 by Shvonne Latrice

All rights reserved.

No part of this book may be reproduced in any form or by any electronic or mechanical means, including information storage and retrieval systems, without written permission from the author, except for the use of brief quotations in a book review.

$14.99
ISBN 978-1-966375-02-9

Morning sickness was a bitch. I loved all my babies, but the beginning process was always so draining. Eating all this food just to throw it up and eat some more. I did enjoy being able to eat whatever I wanted, and being able to send Julius out to obtain my crazy cravings. However, I just wanted to fast forward life to the part where I could keep my food down.

Since I was sick, Winnie decided to take the kids out for a walk at the park. She said she needed the exercise and I needed the break. I was just gonna relax in bed, eat, watch movies, and pray for Lucy. I'd been visiting her every day, but I was too ill to do so today.

BOOM!

I heard the back door open and close, so I assumed Winnie was back. She had just left about fifteen minutes ago, so it was odd that she was back already. I hoped she wasn't though, because I knew my son was gonna be all over me. He was so attached to me. Usually I loved it, but I wasn't in the mood right now.

"Winnie?" I called out. "Winnie?" I called again when I got no answer.

I climbed out of the bed, and then headed down the stairs slowly. I grabbed a knife from the kitchen and walked towards the backdoor. I was so scared that the person who had shot at me had come back to finish the job. I was sure that I was gonna die this time if they did return.

"I missed you baby."

I turned around to see Marlon standing there with a smile on his crazy face. His hair was a mess, and his beard was so long that he reminded me of a black Santa Claus. He was panting heavily, and only had on jeans and a white t-shirt. First, it was crazy ass Frank, and now psycho ass Marlon. I could only imagine how they would act if we would've had sex.

"Marlon, how did you get in my house?" I inquired. *How did he get past the alarm system?* I wondered.

"Someone close to you gave me the code. Don't worry about that though," he grinned as he started to walk toward me.

"What do you want?" I asked clenching the knife in my hands tightly.

"I want you, but I know you're married so I just came to get what I'm owed," he replied licking his dry lips.

"What you're owed?"

"Yeah ma, you owe me some pussy. You strung me along, making me think I'd get some and you never fulfilled that promise," he stared at me seriously. "I want it! I deserve it!" he boomed.

"Marlon, that was a long time ago. Plus, you slept with my best friend!" I said backing away as he came even closer.

"That is your fault! You pushed me away!" he yelled so loud that his voice echoed throughout the mansion.

"Marlon, I don't want to have sex with you," I cried.

"Well then, I will have to take it," he smirked.

"You want to rape me? I deserve that?" I asked trying to stall. I hoped I could think of a plan or that Winnie would come home.

"I'm gonna have to rape you unless you lie down and let me," he folded his arms and pursed his lips. "It's the least you could do since you fucked over my brother," he added.

"Your brother?" I squinted my eyes in confusion.

"Frank, you little hoe," he spat and balled up his fists as he slowly started to come towards me again.

No wonder Marlon had an Indianapolis number when I first met him. What are the odds that I would start dating Frank's brother? That would explain why they both turned psycho.

I was scared as hell, so I ran to the phone to call 911. Marlon pounced on me, and pinned me to the couch, making me drop the knife. I kneed him in the nuts, and he fell back off me and onto the floor. I reached for the phone again, but he grabbed me from behind and pulled me away. He flipped me onto my back and got in between my legs. I dug my nails into his neck and scraped off as much skin as I could. I wanted to rip a damn hole into his neck. Whatever I needed to do to stop him from raping me, I was gonna do it.

"Arrggghhh! You fucking bitch!" he yelled letting me go.

He stared at me as he panted heavily, while holding onto his neck. I tried to dial, but he charged towards me again at full speed. I grabbed the small Keurig machine off the table, and bashed him over the head. He wobbled back a bit but tried to keep coming, so I bashed him again. I kept bashing him over the head until he finally hit the floor. Blood poured from his head as he stared at the ceiling with his eyes bucked. *Did I kill him? Oh shit!* I thought.

"Marlon, get up!" I shouted slapping his face.

I felt for his pulse, and got nothing. *Natalia you just murdered somebody*, I said to myself. I looked around the living room, and blood was everywhere. *Call Julius!* I told myself.

"Natalia! What did you do?"

I snapped my neck to look at the person behind me, and my eyes almost popped out of my head.

"P-Paula?" I furrowed my brows.

"Yes bitch," she chuckled as she snapped photos of me holding a dead Marlon.

"I, umm, I-" I stammered as I stood up, because I had no idea what to say.

"This is perfect," she cackled and put her phone away. "Now you have no choice but to help me off your friend," she raised a brow and put her hand on her hip.

"Paula, I told you I wasn't gonna help you with that! Plus, Lucy is in a coma right now!" I shouted as tears slipped from my eyes.

I had just committed a murder not even five minutes ago so I wasn't in the mood to deal with her jealousy.

"Don't fucking yell at me Natalia! Now like I said, either you help me or I'm showing these photos to the police," she smirked.

"Help you how, Paula?" I sobbed and threw out my bloody hands. "Lucy may not even make it," I added.

"You're gonna help me make sure she *doesn't* make it," she grinned.

What the fuck? Why was I always in some bullshit? If it wasn't someone trying to break Julius and I up, it was another thing. I know one thing--I was tired of being blackmailed. It was either go to jail for killing Marlon, or aid some crazy hoe in killing my best friend. Neither sounded better than the other, so I was stuck between a rock and a hard place.

"So do we have a deal?" Paula snapped her fingers as she moved closer to me.

"Sure," I nodded. I hadn't made up my mind yet, but I was gonna tell her anything to get her out of my face.

"Good, because I didn't want to have to turn you into the police. You're way too pretty so I'm sure the dykes would've had a field day with you in the penitentiary," she laughed loudly and sashayed out the backdoor.

I rushed after her and locked the backdoor. I put the alarm code back on, and then ran back to the area where Marlon was laid out. I didn't know what to do at the moment, but I knew who would.

"Hey beautiful," Julius smiled into the phone.

"Ju, I need you to come home," I sniffled.

"Why babe? I'm in the middle of playing Call of Duty with Lee-"

"Julius just come home right now!" I screamed into the phone.

He was so fucking stupid. I'm obviously crying and his excuse is that he's playing Call of Duty with his dusty ass homeboy?

"A'ight babe, damn," he scoffed and then disconnected.

I tried sitting on the couch, but I was too damn anxious. I ran to the linen closet and got a sheet to put on the floor. Once it was in place, I rolled Marlon onto it because he was staining my carpet. That may be shallow, but it was very nice carpet. After that, I washed my hands and then returned to wait for Julius. I needed him to get here before Winnie and my babies, so I quickly called her and told her to stop at the grocery store for a list of stuff I really didn't need.

"Natalia!" Julius called out as he walked in and then stopped in his tracks. "What the fuck happened Nat?" he asked as he looked on in horror.

"I, umm, he... we got into a fight," I replied as I twiddled my thumbs.

"This was some hell of a fight babe. Is he dead?" Julius inquired as he towered over Marlon's lifeless body. I simply nodded my head yes, once he and I made eye contact.

"Ju, I don't wanna go to jail!" I whined.

"Come here baby, you're not gonna go to jail," he chuckled lightly.

"Are you sure?" I questioned.

"I'm sure babe," he responded before pecking my lips softly. "Go upstairs and clean up, while I get rid of this okay," he huffed and then pulled out his cell phone.

"Okay," I said and then rushed off to take a shower.

Thank God I had a husband like Julius, because any other nigga would've been looking at me wondering what to do.

After I showered, I walked out from the bathroom within our room to find Julius laid out on the bed. I bucked my eyes because I thought he was supposed to be taking care of things.

"What are you doing?" I quizzed, holding my towel up over my body.

"I'm relaxing before Winnie finishes dinner," he laughed.

"Winnie? She's back?" I yelped.

"Yeah baby, come lay down," he patted the bed.

"Julius, what about the mess?" I shouted in a low tone.

"It's all cleaned up," he nodded.

"That fast? I've only been in the shower for thirty minutes," I squinted my eyes in confusion.

"Yeah, and it was done twenty minutes ago. Now come here so I can have sex with my wife before dinner." He got up and walked over to me to remove my towel. "Shit, you made me stop playing the video game, you owe me," he bit his lip. Why did I *owe* everybody?

I smiled up at him as he lifted my naked body to take me over to the bed. As Julius latched his soft lips and tongue onto my clit, I temporarily forgot about Paula and her threats. However, I knew this was just the beginning.

The fact that Natalia murked that Marlon nigga really didn't bother me at all. I was actually happy he was gone, because I didn't want him chasing my wife anymore. On the contrary, I didn't like the fact that Natalia had done it because it was weighing heavily on her conscience. She wasn't a killer, so I would have much rather taken care of him myself. That's what his ass gets for trying to rape my girl though.

I racked my brain as I tried to figure out who gave him the alarm code to our home since Natalia let me know that was how he got in. The only people that knew the code were Natalia, Winnie, and I, so I was beyond confused. I hoped Natalia hadn't given it to any of her chicken head friends.

"Hey honey," Natalia half-smiled, as she laid our daughter Harmony in her swing. She kissed our son Jackson on his head, and then came and sat next to me on the couch.

"How are you feeling?" I asked.

"I don't know," she whispered and shrugged.

"Don't stress yourself baby, it was just self-defense. I don't need you worrying over something that you don't need to worry about, especially with you carrying my baby," I lifted her chin and kissed her pillow soft lips. "What's bothering you?" I quizzed as a single tear ran down her cheek.

"I might go to jail," she sniffled.

"Natalia, no one is gonna find the body trust me." I looked into her eyes so she would know I was serious.

"It's not that Julius," she sobbed and dropped her head into her small hands.

"Then what is it?" I frowned.

"Paula came in, a-and s-she took pictures before you got here. She said she would tell the police if I didn't help her get Rashad back," she cried.

"Paula? She has pictures of the body?" I inquired to be sure and she nodded. *Fuck*, I said to myself.

"I can't be pregnant in jail!" she whimpered.

"Natalia Tate, you are not gonna go to jail. I would never let that happen to you okay?" I said rubbing her long brown hair. "Okay?" I repeated.

"Okay," she smiled and I slipped my tongue into her mouth.

I kissed her passionately, while rubbing my hands on her smooth peanut butter thighs. I loved this girl more than my life, and I'd be damned if I allowed some weirdo hood rat send her to jail. Paula had to go, and I didn't give a fuck who had a problem with it.

After Natalia laid that information on me, it was obvious who gave Marlon's ass the alarm code. I was angry that Natalia had even given it to her but she was dealing with enough shit. Plus, that's just how Natalia was. She was very trusting of anybody that was nice to her. I needed to break her from that shit.

I pulled up to Rashad's crib because I needed to holler at him about his crazy ass ex-girlfriend. I don't know what he did to that hoe, but she had another thing coming if she thought she was about to be threatening Natalia over a nigga. I don't care if that nigga *was* my brother.

"What's up man?" he said dryly as he opened his front door.

"What's up with you?" I asked as I looked around his messy living room. "Nigga you need some Febreze in this bitch, it's smelling like boiled eggs and corn nuts," I turned my nose up.

"Aye, fuck you, nigga, cleaning is the last thing on my mind," he plopped down on the couch and threw his head back.

"What are the doctors saying?" I quizzed.

"They're just saying that they don't know if she and the baby will make it, and that I may have to choose," he replied.

"Where is Lucy's mother?" I frowned.

"Back in Indianapolis. They hadn't really kept in contact since she moved here," he said as he opened up a beer. "You want one?" he offered.

"I'm straight. Look Shad, I need to talk to you about Paula," I stated.

"What about her? I ain't tripping off her," he scoffed.

"Yeah, well I am. She's threatening Nat about that Marlon shit and I'm just letting you know that I'm gone have to take care of her," I spoke honestly.

"Take care of her? What kind of threats is she making man? It can't be to where she needs to die," he furrowed his brows.

"Well in my eyes, it's the only way, because she has pictures of Marlon's body." I shrugged.

"Just send her off somewhere or-"

"I ain't sending shit off no fucking where! I didn't come for your permission. I came to give you a heads up!" I cut in.

"Chill out Ju! Let me talk to her," he said calmly.

"Talk to her? So she can run to the police? No, fuck that! Only thing I need you to do is find out how many pictures she has of the scene and destroy it. Once that's done, I'm gone slide in and take her out," I spat.

"Julius man we-"

"Just do what the fuck I said homie. Shit, she's probably the one who did that shit to Lucy anyway," I shook my head and left quickly.

I hated to argue with my brother, but he needed to understand where I was coming from. This had nothing to do with me, and everything to do with Natalia. Despite my actions in the past, I loved her and my kids with all my heart. I would suffer and die before I let anyone harm her or put her in jail for life. If that caused a wedge between my brother and I, then so be it, but Natalia was number one.

NATALIA

ONE WEEK LATER

"Okay, this is what needs to go into the IV," Paula smiled and handed me a vile.

"So, I just pour it in?" I asked.

"I forgot how dumb you were," she rolled her eyes and then reached into her purse.

I wanted to curse her the fuck out, but I didn't quite have the upper hand here. Julius instructed me to go along with whatever she told me to do until Rashad grew a pair; his words not mine. I didn't tell Julius that her scheme included murdering Lucy; I just said she wanted help in getting Rashad back.

Paula hadn't contacted me since she first prompted me to assist her in killing Lucy, so I thought I was in the clear. That was until she called yesterday telling me *Operation Kill Lucy* would be in full effect.

She stuck a needle into the vile, and filled it up with whatever was in it. She nodded her head as an evil smile crept across her face. This bitch was crazy.

"Here Nat," she said as she handed me a Ziploc bag holding the needle. "Just jam this anywhere into her body and it should do the trick," she added.

"Okay, be right back," I half-smiled and quickly hopped out of the car.

I walked into the hospital slowly, and for some reason, I felt like everyone knew I had this little needle in my purse. I checked in at the front, and received a name badge. *I probably should've used another name*, I thought. I got up to the Intensive Care Unit, and walked to Lucy's area. I brought the curtain around so that we could have some privacy, and then sat next to her bed.

"Hey," I whispered.

I grabbed her hand in mine, and rubbed it. She looked dead and it was heartbreaking to see. I laid her hand next to her body, and then slowly rubbed her stomach. I knew what the doctors told Rashad and I prayed he chose to save her. I know it was selfish of me, but I needed Lucy to stay alive. I didn't even know this baby!

Paula: Hurry the fuck up!

After reading the text, I threw my phone back into my purse and then took the needle out. *What am I gonna do?* I wondered. I couldn't kill Lucy. I looked over at the trashcan and smiled. I pushed all the contents out into the wastebasket, and then threw the needle in. *Wait, she may want some verification.* I told myself before reaching back in to get it.

"Bye Lucy." I kissed her forehead and rushed out before Paula ran her thirsty ass off to the police station.

"Did you do it?" Paula quizzed.

"Yeah," I replied dryly as I buckled my seatbelt.

"Where is the needle? And it better be empty," she scowled.

I stared at her for a couple seconds, and then went into my purse to retrieve the Ziploc bag containing the empty needle. She snatched it from me, and took the needle out of the bag to make sure.

"Cool, she better be gone soon or it's your ass," she said and then gunned it out of the hospital parking lot.

Once I got home, I immediately went to find Winnie and check on my babies. Once I saw that they were okay, I went to the bedroom to find Julius. I saw all four of his cars in the garage, so I knew he was here.

"How did your time with Paula go?" he asked as he stood there with a towel around his waist.

His perfectly chiseled abs and chest glistened. The sight of his strong arms made my body quiver at the thought of them being wrapped around me. He was way too sexy for his own good.

"I need to tell you something," I fidgeted.

"What?" he frowned.

"So Paula wants me to help her bump Lucy off. She gave me a needle filled with something, and told me to inject it into Lucy," I replied.

"What the fuck? Well, what the fuck happened?" he questioned.

"I just threw it out, but I told her I did it. But she said if Lucy isn't dead soon, it's my ass," I started to cry.

"Stop, stop Natalia," he neared me and then pulled me into his lap as he sat on the chair in our room. "Paula ain't gone do shit. I got you," he said in a low tone as he wiped the two tears that ran down my cheeks.

I draped my arms over his shoulders, and tugged his soft bottom lip into my mouth. He ran his big hands up and down my small back, before reaching under my dress and squeezing my ass cheeks. I raised both of my hands in the air, as he pulled my dress over my head and tossed it to the floor, while tonguing me down. He ripped my red lace thong to shreds, before tossing it to the floor as well.

"Ride it," he demanded as he opened his towel. His hard eleven inches sprang up, ready to fill me up.

I mounted it, and then slowly slid down, while digging my nails into his smooth peanut butter shoulders.

"Uggh," I grunted softly and followed it with a whimper.

"All the way down Nat," he ordered as he looked down at his dick going into me.

"Mmmm," I purred as I sat all the way down on his rod.

He pulled my nipple into his mouth, as I moved extremely slow. He cupped my ass cheeks, while switching between my two hard nipples.

"Ride that shit Nat." He bit his lip and laid his head back to watch. "Good job baby," he cheered softly, and spanked my ass.

"I'm about to cum Ju," I cooed as I placed my hand on his hard abs for leverage.

"Cum for daddy." He squinted his sexy brown eyes up at me. "And you better keep eye contact with me," he added while rubbing his hand down my stomach.

"Ahhhh," I released on his pole while staring deeply into his eyes.

He smirked and then took me to the bed, putting me on my back. He flicked his tongue over my nipples, and then kissed down my still flat stomach until he reached my pussy. He licked slowly between the slit, and then let his tongue toy with my clit.

"Juuu," I moaned as I rubbed his fresh fade.

He pushed my legs back a little, and then attacked my clit like he hadn't eaten in days. He darted his tongue into my hole, and then trailed his tongue up to my clit to suck on it. I gripped the comforter, as my chest heaved up and down because of the pleasure. He reached up to play with my hard nipples, while sucking on my button for dear life.

"Uhhh, uhhhh!" I cried out as I released every bit of me into his mouth.

"So sweet Natalia," he whispered as he continued to work his magic between my hips.

He put his hands on the back of my thighs to keep them pushed back, while he sucked and licked me damn near into a coma. My legs trembled as I felt another orgasm rise through my body.

"Fuck Ju," I whimpered as a tear slipped out my eye. I came so hard that my body jerked violently.

He lapped up my juices, and then kissed my lower lips gently making me shiver.

"That pussy is sweet Nat," he smirked and wiped my nectar from his full lips. I panted heavily and couldn't respond. "Don't quit yet baby, daddy gotta nut too," he chuckled as he wiggled his way inside me.

"Shit," he grunted as he pounded into me. His sex faces were the sexiest things on this Earth.

He pinned my hands behind my head and then went faster, making us both scream to the high heavens.

"Listen at how wet you are." He bit his lip as he looked down to watch himself penetrate me repeatedly. I'm sure you could hear him ramming into me around the world.

"Ahhh, uhhh, uggghhh!" we both called out together as we came hard as hell.

He collapsed on top of me, and tongued me down for what seemed like a beautiful eternity. He finally pulled out of me, and then dropped down to kiss between my legs passionately.

"I just had to thank it with a kiss real quick," he joked and we laughed.

JULIUS

Once I told Rashad that Paula was trying to implement Natalia in finishing off Lucy, he was all for killing her ass. I was gonna get this bitch either way, but it felt much better having him on my side. On top of the fact that she tried to get Natalia to kill Lucy, we found out after doing some digging, why her daughter, Gabby's father wasn't around.

Paula told Rashad that he was a deadbeat and ran off when he found out she was pregnant, but that wasn't the case whatsoever. She trapped the nigga just like she was trying to do my brother, and when he found out, he was willing to help but not be with her. She wasn't having that shit, so the bitch lied to her brother and said he raped her. Long story short, her brother killed the nigga *and* his new bitch, and got a life sentence. He died two years after being in the pen though, so we didn't have to worry about him trying to retaliate.

Anyway, when Rashad and I found this out, we knew she had to go. I guess since we ain't originally from here, that was something we wouldn't know. It's funny, because as soon as we started asking about her, niggas were bucking their eyes and shaking their heads before even saying anything. I knew right then that her ass had a background.

Currently, Rashad was in Paula's house laying on the charm. He needed to get all the information he could out of her ass, to make sure she didn't have any extra pictures of Natalia's little mishap. We chose today, because Rashad said every Wednesday Paula took her daughter to her mother's crib.

Anyway, once he shot me that text, I was gonna run up in there and handle her. I could've had my little niggas do this, but this was a sensitive ass matter. We didn't have any room for mistakes or fuck ups when it was regarding my family.

Rashad: *At the store*

I nodded my head at the coded text, and then exited the car. It was around 11pm so no one was really outside like that. I wore all black, and made sure my hood was extra-large to cover my face if need be.

KNOCK

KNOCK

KNOCK

"I got it," I heard Rashad say.

"Did you call someone over?" Paula asked and I could tell by the sound of her voice that she'd been crying.

Rashad opened the door for me, and I strutted in with a smile on my face.

"What the fuck is he doing here?" Paula spat and glared at me.

"Where are the pictures Rashad?" I quizzed.

"Only on her phone, her dumb ass didn't think to make extras. She hasn't told anybody either," Rashad replied as he lifted her phone and laptop up.

PHEW

PHEW

I quickly blew her head open, and then texted Leese and Dash to let them know it was done. Once they came and did their job, we all assisted in wiping the place down and making it look like no one had ever came home that night, not even Paula.

"Aye man, I'm sorry I was tripping," Rashad said to me as I walked to my car.

"It's cool. I'm just glad you came to your senses," I chuckled, and we dapped each other up.

"Well, I'm about to go up to the hospital. I'll check you later. Apologize to Natalia for me," he pursed his lips and then jogged to his car.

"Fasho," I replied.

Once I got home, I immediately torched Paula's belongings in the backyard. Any data or pictures she had, were sure to be gone after that one. *Finally, we can go back to living in peace,* I thought. Then again, we still needed Lucy and the baby to pull through.

I walked into the bedroom quietly, and saw my beautiful wife sleeping soundly. I took a quick shower, and then threw on some boxers before climbing into bed behind her. I wrapped my arms around her small body, and then rubbed her still flat stomach. I kissed the nape of her neck, and inhaled the scent of the soap she used. I could tell she had just taken a bath. I squeezed her tightly as I silently thanked God for her.

"I'm still sore Ju," she slurred in a low tone.

"I'm not trying to have sex babe," I chuckled.

She reached her hand around, and pulled my face to kiss her lips. Our kissing became heavy, and she turned to lie on her back. Initially I wasn't gonna try to fuck, but now my dick was hard. I ran my hand up her dewy thigh, and began to massage her pussy.

"Now I wanna eat it," I whispered in between kisses.

"Ju no, my legs are too sore to open," she giggled as I tugged her thong down.

I ignored her pleas and got down between her legs. I inhaled the scent of her kitten, and then pecked it softly. I kissed it repeatedly, and a soft moan escaped her mouth. I inhaled the scent again before diving in and sucking extremely gently. I let her legs rest on my shoulders since she said she was sore. I gripped her small waist, and closed my eyes to enjoy the feast.

NATALIA

Now that Julius had taken care of Paula, it was much easier for me to sleep at night. I was worried about her daughter Gabby, but Julius made me feel better when he said she was with her grandmother Sandra. I knew Sandra would be calling me soon, however, to question if I'd seen or heard from Paula, and I was not looking forward to that. Good thing she knew that we had stopped being friends, because that would support me telling her no.

Committing a murder still bothered me every now and then too. At first, I still felt bad about what I had done to Marlon because he was a nice guy, but then I had to remind myself of what he had come there to do. Also, the fact that he was Frank's brother let me know that he initially had an ulterior motive when trying to get with me. I didn't quite know what it was, but I didn't care either.

I was relaxing in the backyard by the pool in my new orange swimsuit called SAM. I just ordered it from Draya's Mint Swim line, and was extremely excited to wear it. My stomach wouldn't be as flat in a couple months, so I needed to take advantage. Julius had gone to the grocery store to pick up some meat because we were gonna have a little intimate family barbecue.

"Mrs. Tate your phone," Winnie said as she walked into the back area by the pool.

"Are my babies still asleep?" I asked as I moved my shades up and took the phone.

"Yes," she smiled and then jogged back into the house. Maury must've been on, which was why she was rushing.

"Hello?" I said into the phone, remembering that I'd forgotten to ask Winnie who it was.

"Natalia, hi." The voice sounded like my mother but I knew it wasn't her. It couldn't be her; she never called me.

Ever since my mother, or Dalia, kicked me out of her house three years ago, she hasn't cared about me, or what I was doing. She didn't even know that I moved to South Carolina until Julius flew her out to our wedding. Whenever I called her, she acted as if I was bothering her unless she needed a check, so eventually I gave up on our relationship.

"Dalia?" I quizzed not believing it was her.

"Yes honey, hi," she exhaled heavily.

"Oh, umm, how are you?" I asked.

"I'm not doing too well," she replied.

"What's wrong?" I questioned and sat up.

I was waiting for her to ask me to write a check. I never wanted to give her money, but Julius always advised me just to do it.

"I'm sick baby," she coughed into the phone, and I pulled it back some because it was loud.

"Sick with what?"

"I have ovarian cancer. Good thing I had you when I did," she joked but it wasn't funny. She was only thirty-five years old, and had plenty of time to have more children in my book.

"Dalia, I can come see you. Or better yet, you should come stay with Julius and I," I said hoping he would be okay with it.

"Is there enough room?" she inquired.

"Yeah, there is plenty. We have two guestrooms outside of the four that are being used now," I beamed.

"I don't have the funds to come out there Natalia," she huffed.

"Don't worry about it Dalia, I will buy your ticket," I smiled waiting for her response. I didn't know why I was smiling at the thought of seeing her.

"When? I could die any minute," she stated.

"I will buy it right now, so it should be a flight for tomorrow," I responded.

"Great. I'm too weak to pack so I will need all new things," she coughed and then disconnected before I could respond.

I couldn't say I wasn't excited to see my mother. Although she treated me badly, I still loved her. She didn't have her mother, so maybe that's why she couldn't do a good job being a mother to me. Whatever it was, I wasn't gonna penalize her for it, especially when she may not have that long to live.

I rushed into the house to purchase a plane ticket for my mom. I knew I should've asked Julius first, but if he loved me, then he shouldn't have a problem with it. But if he did, all I had to do was give him some and it'd shut him up for a little bit. I wasn't worried about him hitting me because he kept his promise that he wouldn't, and that was over a year ago. Boy have we come a long way. I can remember when being cheated on and abused was a normal thing for me. I was glad that he changed though, because I really loved his crazy ass. I would've hated to leave him, but I would have definitely done so.

"What?" Julius frowned as we sat in the Jacuzzi. We'd all just eaten barbecue, and decided to relax for a little bit while Jackson and Harmony played with their toys.

"Promise you won't get upset," I smiled.

"Nope," he replied.

"Pleeeaase," I pouted playfully and he chuckled.

"What the fuck you do man?" he questioned.

"Dalia is sick, a-and I told her she could come stay with us," I quickly spit it out.

"Sick? What kind of sick?" he inquired.

"She has cancer in her ovaries," I nodded somberly.

"Damn babe. Well, when is she coming?"

"Tomorrow afternoon," I grinned.

"I'm not upset, but next time you need to ask me when making decisions like that, aight?" he raised a brow.

"Yes daddy," I replied and pecked his lips.

He pulled me closer to him so that I was straddling his lap in the Jacuzzi. We sucked one another's lips, and let our tongues dance together.

"I love you, Ju," I whispered while cupping his smooth face.

"I love you more Natalia," he responded in between kisses.

Hopefully, being around family would make my mother feel better. I didn't know how far along the cancer was, but I was gonna pray very hard to make sure that she was okay.

JULIUS

Now that I had taken over Orangeburg, South Carolina *and* kept my hold on Indianapolis, I had to split my connects. At first, I had them both shipping to both states, but now it seemed to be too much. I decided to keep Bart sending shipments to South Carolina, and then have Antonio ship to Indiana. It was gonna call for a lot flying back and forth, but I wasn't tripping. As long as I was getting this money, I didn't care what it took.

I pulled up to Bart's house, because he said he had a new schedule to give me now that the changes were in place. This nigga was living very well, especially now that I was his sole distributor for South Carolina.

"Julius." Bart's daughter, Skylar opened the door.

I low-key wished this nigga would've told me she was gonna be here because I would've met him somewhere else. A part of me felt like he wanted me with his daughter though. Skylar's ass had been on me ever since I met her in Los Angeles years ago. No matter how many times I turned that pussy down, she was persistent with it. I don't even think she wanted to be with me. I think she just wanted to get dicked down behind Natalia's back every now and then. What she failed to realize was if I wouldn't fuck her back then, I damn sure ain't gonna do it now.

It wasn't like she wasn't attractive because she was very attractive. She was half-Spanish and half-black, with a body to die for. But, like I told her plenty of times, I'm a married man and I plan to be faithful to my wife. I put her through enough shit, and she still loved me after it all. Natalia deserved someone who would be good to her, and that was gonna be me. Just the thought of another man treating her the way she deserved, made my blood boil. Plus, I wasn't even interested in other women. I've fucked so many bitches during my life, that I had a pretty good idea of what was out there, and it wasn't shit.

"What's up, where is your father?" I asked as I walked into the foyer.

"He will be down in a minute. Would you like something to drink?" she smiled and folded her arms over her large breasts.

"Nah, I'm straight. Where should I wait?" I questioned.

"Follow me," she smirked and started to walk towards the back.

"Cool. Let him know I'm here and I ain't got all day," I told her as I sat down on the couch.

"Yes sir!" she joked and left out.

I checked my text messages and replied to a couple of them as I waited. I was serious about having something else to do. Today, Natalia and I were gonna go check on the progress of her cupcake bakery. My baby girl was excited and I knew that I couldn't be late.

"He said he is coming." Skylar re-entered the room and sat at the other end of the couch. I didn't say anything in response. "So how have you been?" she beamed.

"The same since you saw me last," I replied dryly.

"Damn, oh me? I've been great. Thanks for asking," she said sarcastically and again, I didn't respond. "I guess I'm boring you," she chuckled after seeing me look at my watch.

"I just have something to do after this. I told you that," I exhaled heavily.

"You look nice today Ju," she scooted closer to me. "What cologne is that? I smelled it on another guy and immediately thought of you," she added.

"Skylar, please leave me alone. Can't you take a hint?" I frowned. There was no reason for a girl as pretty as her to be this damn thirsty.

"And can't you see that I'm tireless?" she raised a brow and licked her thin lips.

"I'm sure there are plenty of single guys that would love to be with you. There really is no need for you to be chasing after me. It's never gonna happen," I shook my head.

"I don't care about other guys; I care about you. And never say never boo." She touched my hand and I snatched it away just as Bart entered the room.

"Julius, hey," Bart smiled as Skylar got off the couch.

"We were just bonding daddy," Skylar said and Bart winked. "I'll bring you guys some iced tea," she added before floating off.

"Sorry about that," Bart chuckled.

"Man, you doing that shit on purpose," I scoffed.

"Maybe, but you can't prove it," he laughed.

"I'm a married man, what are you trying to do? You know I'm on the thinnest ice possible with Natalia." I ran my hand over my face.

"Hey, Skylar has her own brain. I'm not telling her to like you. Plus, you need to be able to hide from your wife," he nodded.

"It ain't even about me getting caught. I know how not to get caught. I just- why are we even talking about this? Where is the new schedule so I can be up out of here?" I turned my lip up.

Bart shook his head as he snickered, then picked up a manila folder. He looked through some papers and then handed me one of them.

"So, since we have two cities solely now, the shipments will come Monday, Wednesday, and Thursday instead of just Monday, and a half shipment on Thursdays," he said.

"These are all full shipments now right?" I asked to be sure and he nodded.

"Aight, peace," I said as I hopped up to leave the den area.

As I was walking out, I almost bumped into Skylar with the tray of iced tea.

"Excuse me," I said before quickly walking around.

"Only a matter of time Julius. I know your kind," she called after me as I booked it to their front door.

I was a changed man, and there was no way any woman on this Earth was gonna get me to cheat on Natalia. These hoes made me sick to my stomach.

"Clayton it looks so good already," Natalia beamed.

"Yeah, we really wanted to make sure you had a nice size display case, and a huge kitchen like you asked," he replied.

"Yes, I appreciate that. So how much longer?" she asked as she looked around the partially built kitchen.

"Two and a half to three months," he nodded as he eyed the place.

"Not bad," Natalia smiled at me and I smiled back.

"Are you excited?" I quizzed once we were in the car.

"Yes, thank you baby." She leaned over for a kiss while we were stopped at a red light.

"You deserve it. I'm sure you're gonna make way more money than what I'm putting into the place," I responded, pulling off.

"I hope so. Oh, the nurse that they're sending for my mother is $4000 a month. Is that okay?" she questioned as we pulled into our roundabout driveway. "I can tell them-"

"Nah, it's fine babe. I'm your man, I got you," I said before planting a soft kiss on her full lips.

"Thank you," she half-smiled as she stared into my eyes. I touched her stomach and gave her a kiss with a little bit more passion.

Everything in my life was going great, except for the fact that my best friend was laid up in the hospital. On the positive side, she had finally awakened from the coma. I was so excited to see her and tell her all the things that were happening in my life.

"Hello Natalie!" the nurse receptionist smiled as I approached the desk.

"It's Nuh-tal-ya," I corrected her and we chuckled.

"Oh, I'm sorry honey. Here is your sticker to go up and see Ms. Ouistin," she said as she handed the sticker badge over to me.

"It's okay, and thank you," I replied and headed to the elevator.

Lucy was now in her own room, away from the rest of the Intensive Care Unit patients. I stopped at her door and took a deep breath. I started to cough because I inhaled the strong scent of the roses I purchased for her. I knocked lightly before walking in, and I saw her staring at the ceiling. It felt so good to see her alive and well.

"Lucy," I whispered and cheesed.

"Natalia," she half- smiled and reached her arms out to me.

I power walked over to her and hugged her tightly. We embraced one another in silence for a couple moments, before I finally pulled away.

"How are you?" I questioned as I pulled a chair up next to her bed.

"I've been better," she shrugged and sipped the ice water that was near her.

"What? You're alive and the person who did this isn't," I smiled and handed over the roses once I realized I was still holding them.

"And neither is my baby," she looked at me and a tear slipped down her light cheek.

"Y-you lost the baby?" I quizzed although she'd just told me she did. She nodded her head, and then pressed it up against her pillow. "I'm so sorry Lucy." I grabbed her hand in mine.

"It's okay. I wasn't even pregnant that long," she chuckled nervously.

"You can still be sad," I frowned.

"Yeah?" she raised a brow.

"Of course," I nodded. "Where are Rashad and Lumar?" I inquired as I looked around the room.

"Well, they're at home. Rashad took the death of the baby really hard, so he can only stay for an hour or two," she exhaled.

"I'm sure you guys will be fine," I half-smiled. I didn't really know if they would, since something like this had never happened to me. I prayed that they could make it though.

I sat and talked with Lucy for about three hours, then remembered I needed to get home. Today, the in-home nurse we hired for my mother was coming over. I was excited to meet her and feel her out. In the email that I received pertaining to her background, I saw that she was only twenty-six years old. I would've preferred someone older, but the agency we used said she was really good, and I trusted them.

"The nurse will be here soon Dalia," I told my mother.

"Tell that Winifred she needs to learn to make a bed properly," she spat, ignoring my statement.

"Winnie? She makes the beds good in my opinion," I shrugged as I leaned up against the door.

"Well, we all know how flawed your opinion is Natalia," she fake smiled, and then laughed to herself as she ran her hands across the comforter.

"Just come to the good living room when you're finished," I rolled my eyes and left out.

After raining kisses and tickles all over my babies, Winnie finally let me know that the young nurse was here to meet my mother and I.

"Hello," I grinned as I walked into the good living room.

We called it the "good living room" because it was the room where Julius and I didn't allow lounging or the kids to play. We only held small meetings or entertained guests in it.

"Hi Mrs. Tate, I'm River York," she smiled.

River was very pretty. She had a caramel complexion like myself, but was very skinny. I was small too, but she was like a surfboard in the assets department. Her hair was a golden blond color and pinned up into a tight knit bun. She had on navy blue scrubs and some ugly white sneakers.

"River, that is a pretty name. My mother, Dalia will be in here in a second. Sit down," I said and we both sat on the couches across from each other.

Dalia walked in finally, and sat down next to me, and then Winnie walked in with some tea. After pouring us all a cup, she left the room so we could talk.

"River, this is my mother Dalia. Dalia, River York," I introduced them.

"Nice to meet you Dalia." She smiled at my mother. "Mrs. Tate, I just have to say you are extremely beautiful," River shook her head as she stared at me in awe.

"Really?" I frowned. "I mean, thank you. You can call me Natalia by the way," I chuckled and my mother rolled her eyes.

"So how long are you gonna be here per day?" my mom asked.

"Well, I will come five days a week and seven hours each day," River replied.

"You look kind of young; do you know what you're doing?" my mother raised a brow.

"Yes ma'am. I am very knowledgeable, and you don't have to worry about anything." River giggled at my mom's forward ass questions.

"Don't call me ma'am. Call me Dalia. I'm only thirty-five, way too young to be called ma'am," she said as she stood up. "Are we done here? My soaps are on," she frowned.

"Yeah, sure Dalia, I will finish up here," I shook my head and she switched out.

"Your mom is funny," River sipped her tea. "So I saw that you had a husband, is he here?" she asked.

"Yes, his name is Julius," I responded.

"Wow he must be great," she smirked.

"Why do you say that?" I quizzed.

"Because, you blushed when you said his name," she beamed and we both giggled.

I was happy we got along, especially because she was gonna be around so much. I didn't like that she asked about Julius though. If she had any ideas of sleeping with my nigga, she needed to get it out of her head now.

JULIUS

"Ju, come meet Dalia's nurse," Natalia walked into the bedroom. She looked so pretty in an orange dress. I loved when she wore orange because it brought out her honey skin tone. Her long brown hair was in a low bun, and she had no makeup on, just the way I liked her.

"What do I need to meet her for?" I smirked.

"She's really nice. Plus, don't you wanna know who you're paying $4000 to?" she folded her arms and poked out her little hip.

"That money is coming out of the joint account," I lied to fuck with her.

"It is?" she bucked her eyes.

"I'm fucking with you greedy. I will be down in a minute," I kissed her lips and she smiled before rushing out.

I slipped on some gray sweats, a black t-shirt, and some black Jordan Retro 1's. I was just meeting up with my boys today, so there was no need to dress up and shit. I brushed my waves, and then grabbed my car keys before walking down to Dalia's room.

"Knock, knock," I said as I lightly tapped on the cracked door.

"Oh River, this is my husband Julius," Natalia hopped up and rushed over to me cheesing.

"Good looking couple. Nice to meet you Mr. Tate," River stuck her hand out and I shook it.

"Likewise River. Well, take good care of mother-in-law," I said before turning on my heels.

"Don't stay out too long, I'm making chicken tacos tonight," Natalia smiled up at me with her pretty ass.

"My favorite. I'll be back in time." I pecked her soft lips and then put up the peace sign to Dalia and River.

Something about that nurse seemed strange, but it could just be my paranoia. I didn't trust anybody really, but hopefully she was legit. The agency we hired her from is A1 though, so I shouldn't be too worried I guess.

"Now the shipments will come three days a week since we're supplying both Charleston and Orangeburg from just Bart," I explained to my team as I had them pass a paper around to look at it.

"Can we get copies?" my worker Alonzo asked.

"Hell no," I turned my lip up and shook my head at him. "If you need a fucking copy to remember this shit, then you need to rock with somebody else," I spat.

"Nah, I meant for everybody else. I'm good boss," he nodded.

"So does anybody have any questions?" I asked the room. It was only five of us in there because only certain people dealt with the shipments.

"I'm straight," everyone said randomly.

"Rashad?" I raised my brow at him. He'd been quiet the whole time, staring at the ground.

"Yeah," he replied barely above a whisper.

I knew he was going through it because his unborn child had passed, but I really needed him to be on his shit. I had a lot of territory and I needed him to be on his toes and help me out. On top of running three areas, I had my club and winery to run. Natalia was a big help, but she had her bakery to look over and it was only gonna get worse when it actually opened.

"Aight, this meeting is adjourned." I patted the long wooden table and everyone got up to leave.

"Aye Julius, can we holla at you?" Jabari and Luke said once the room was clear.

"What's good?" I quizzed.

"Remember when we told you we used to work for a nigga named Brax?" Luke asked me and I nodded. "Well he's being released from jail in a couple weeks, and word on the street is that he's coming back to take over," Luke finished.

"Is that right?" I squinted my eyes.

"Yeah," Jabari replied and nodded.

"Well, I ain't really worried about no washed up ass kingpin trying to reclaim his throne. I'll cross that bridge when I get to it. That's if it even gets built," I said standing up.

"And just to let you know, we're fucking with you," Jabari smiled and Luke nodded.

"I know. I didn't think otherwise," I smiled.

Brax is hilarious. I heard he was really making moves when he was free, so if anything, I would offer him the chance to work for me. If he declined then he would just go hungry, there would be no takeover. Hopefully, he didn't have to learn the hard way. I would be more than happy to make an example out him if he tried to stir the pot though.

As I was walking out of my office building, my phone buzzed in my pocket. I retrieved it, and saw it was a text from an un-stored number. This was my work phone so I wasn't alarmed because I got texts from un-stored numbers all the time.

(843) 555- 3151: Have a goodnight boo.

I jerked my neck back because now I *was* alarmed. The only people that text this work phone were niggas, and I was hoping nobody was on that gay shit.

Me: You are?

(843) 555-3151: Skylar, your future wife.

I quickly blocked her number, and deleted our conversation.

When I said I wasn't gonna entertain these hoes, I meant it. My wife knew the code to both of my phones, and I didn't want to risk her seeing this conversation, or seeing this hoe calling.

This nigga Bart was pissing me off, because I knew he gave her my number. He only has my work number so that explains why she texted this phone. Why did he even want his daughter fucking with a married man? I wouldn't dare try to force my baby girl Harmony on some married nigga, especially one with *my* track record.

I drove home thinking about all the shit I had on my back. I really needed another vacation, but I wanted to wait until everybody was straight. When I say everybody, I mean my brother and his girl, and then this whole Brax shit.

I pulled up to my crib, and my stomach growled at the thought of the tacos my wife made. I walked into the house from the garage, and quickly went to wash my hands so I could eat. I heard some voices, including my son and daughter's coming from the dining room, which put a smile on my face. After I took a piss and cleaned my hands, I entered the dining area to see Natalia, Winnie, Dalia, my kids, and that nurse bitch River at the table.

"Here babe," Natalia patted the chair next to her.

"We ain't paying you for this are we?" I asked River as I took a seat next to my wife.

"Ju!" Natalia yelped.

"Are we?" I repeated and looked at her ass with my brow raised.

Shit if she said yes, she had to take her food to go. It wasn't that I didn't have it because I obviously did, but she wasn't about to get extra money from me while eating my food! She better be checking someone's blood pressure in between bites or some shit.

"No, Natalia asked me to stay for dinner," River smiled and bit her taco.

"Aight," I said as kissed Natalia's lips.

"**A**hhh Juu," Natalia moaned as I gripped her small waist. I thrust into her from the back, while rotating my hips in a circular motion. I lifted and spread her ass cheeks so I could get a better view of myself going in and out of her. I bit my bottom lip as I watched her juices coat my dick, while feeling her tight pussy contract around my rod.

"Shit," I panted and smacked her smooth ass.

"Mmmm," she purred as she looked over her shoulder at me. We made eye contact, which caused my nut to start rising.

"I'm about to nut babe! Fuck!" I whimpered like a bitch as I beat it up.

"Ugghhh!" we both grunted as we came.

I bent down and pulled her lip into my mouth, before slipping my tongue into hers. As we were kissing hungrily, the door burst open.

"Can y'all quiet the fuck down! I'm tired of listening to this shit every night!" Dalia shouted as she stood in the doorway.

Natalia and I were frozen in the doggy style position, as the three of us stared at each other. I slowly slid out of Natalia and quickly covered my dick with the sheet. Natalia covered her small body, and swallowed the lump in her throat.

"S-sorry Dalia," she finally replied.

Dalia rolled her eyes chuckling, and then left the room. I immediately burst into laughter and Natalia smacked my arm.

"We can't have sex while she's here," Natalia whispered.

"Yes we can, and we will," I scoffed and checked my phone. I got up and then walked around to her side of the bed. I picked her up bridal style, and carried her to the bathroom within our room. "We can just do it here," I said as I turned the Jacuzzi tub on.

"Okay," she smiled seductively and closed the bathroom door.

TWO WEEKS LATER

My mom had become extremely annoying, but I just had to remind myself that she was bitter. She was too young to be that way, however. All she did was complain about everything and everyone. I wanted to talk to her because with me being pregnant, I didn't need anyone stressing me out.

"Good morning Dalia," I said as I walked into her room. It was around 9am and I wanted to talk to her before River arrived.

"Morning," she coughed and then paused the DVR. Although she was sick, her smooth brown skin was still flawless, and her brown hair was thick and long.

"I just wanted to talk to you," I smiled and then sat down on the edge of her bed.

"About what? I'm not in the mood to be bothered Natalia," she rolled her eyes.

"I just want you to calm down and not be so negative," I stated.

"Not be so negative? What is going on in my life to where I should be positive?" she quizzed.

"You're not dead, and-"

"And what? Nothing else! I'm on my way to being dead, and I'm living with my daughter and her drug dealing husband," she shouted.

"Don't talk that way about Julius," I huffed.

"Julius, Julius, Julius. Is that all you give a fuck about? I wish you hadn't ended up with someone like him," she shook her head in disgust. "You deserve better baby."

"I used to wish that too, but that was years ago Dalia. Julius is different, and he loves me," I replied.

"Loves you? You don't know what love is little girl," she smacked her lips.

"You're right Dalia. When I first met him, I didn't know what love was, but you know why? I'd never experienced being loved or cared about, so the first person that showed me anything, I hopped on. You didn't care about me, so yeah, Julius may have been a bad guy but one thing I could say was that he cared," I sobbed.

"Natalia, I cared honey."

"No! No you didn't! I was a burden to you! After you kicked me out when I was pregnant, you never once tried to find out what happened to me! If it wasn't for Julius, it's no telling where I would even be! So the next time you wanna trash his character, remember that he loved and cared for your child even when you didn't!" I spat and then rushed out before she could say anything.

I hated to yell at my mother but she deserved it. She had some nerve acting like she was the greatest parent ever. We all knew that Julius and I had problems in the past, but he was the only person who was willing to care for me. My mother didn't even buy me food, yet Julius always made sure I was fed. I was so used to fending for myself and taking care of my best friend, so it felt good to meet someone who expected nothing from me and was willing to care for me. I'd never even heard the words *I love you,* until I met Julius. So yes, me being sixteen years old, of course I was gonna fall for him despite his ways. Regardless of the past, I wasn't gonna allow anyone to talk about my husband, because for a long time he treated me better than most of the people I knew, and he still does.

After cleaning my face, I pulled out my phone to text Julius.

Me: *I love you.*

Husband: *I love you too baby.*

I smiled at the text, and then went to feed and bathe Jackson and Harmony. Once I was done with them I was famished, so I went downstairs to see what Winnie had made for lunch.

After I finished eating a huge homemade chicken salad, it was time for a nap. As I was walking past the bathroom, I heard someone sniffling. I lightly tapped on the door, and waited for an answer. I heard rustling, and then the knob jiggled signaling that the person behind it was unlocking it.

"Oh, I'm sorry Natalia. I was just-"

"River, why are you crying?" I frowned.

"Oh it's nothing," she shrugged.

"Come on, tell me," I half-smiled.

"I just broke up with my boyfriend," she sobbed.

"Don't cry, River." I chuckled inside at the irony of her name being River, and me telling her not to cry. "I'm sure he wasn't good enough for you anyways," I smacked my lips and she laughed.

"You think so?" she cocked her head.

"I know so. The person you're meant to be with is probably waiting somewhere right now," I joked and we chuckled.

"Thank you Natalia, I appreciate that," she sniffled.

"It's cool," I smiled.

"Have you and Julius ever broken up?" she inquired, as I was about to walk away.

"Umm, not really. We've had a couple snags, but we have always been together pretty much," I replied.

"I see," she nodded and then walked to go back downstairs to my mother's room.

JULIUS

I heard Natalia downstairs in the laundry room, and I knew this was the perfect opportunity for some midday. She was always thinking about her mother bursting in on us, so she only wanted to do it at night. However, a nigga like me needed it all day and any time of the damn day.

I rushed down the stairs, and power walked to the damn laundry room. As soon as I reached it, I closed the door behind me. Natalia had on some little ass shorts and a tube top. When she bent over, I ain't gone even get into all that. I crept up behind her, and rubbed my hard dick on her ass. I was still fully clothed, but my dick was threatening to rip through my sweats.

"Ju, we can't," she giggled as she turned around to look up at me.

"Yes we can," I replied as I lifted her onto the washing machine.

I yanked her tube top down to expose her small round breasts, and took one of her hard nipples into my mouth. She pulled up on my shirt, so I allowed her to remove it before latching back onto her nipples. I unbuttoned her jean shorts, and pulled them to her ankles, along with her thin lace thong. After dropping my sweats and boxers, Natalia dropped down to her knees and began to tease the tip of my dick.

"Shit," I grunted lightly.

I massaged her scalp gently, while she worked her mouth up and down my shaft. The feeling of her soft lips on my dick was almost too much to bear. Her saliva was soaking my dick, and her mouth was so warm.

"Look at you," I whispered as I stared down at her sexy ass sucking my dick. I loved seeing her suck my dick butt naked. "Mmmm," I released down her throat, and she swallowed it up like the little freak that she was.

I bent her over the washer, and slowly slid into her sopping wet pussy. I reached my hand around to play with her clit, and she spread her legs some more.

"Juuuu, ahhhh," she purred as I slid in fast and pulled out slowly.

Her little fat ass was bouncing and turning me on to the fucking max. I swear she was so damn sexy and I knew she didn't even try.

"Mm," I grunted as I spanked her ass.

"Uhh," she cried out in pain and pleasure as she exploded on my dick.

I gripped her waist tightly, and slammed into her at a faster pace. The sounds of our skin smacking seemed like the greatest soundtrack in the world. I reached down and grabbed a handful of her long brown hair, then wrapped it around my hand. I gripped her hair as I pumped into her soaking wet center.

"Fuck, Juuu," she whimpered before we both came together.

I turned her around, bent her head back, and then slipped my tongue into her mouth. I sucked on her soft lips and she sucked on mine. I smacked her ass and then gently bit her bottom lip.

"See, I'm sure you needed that just as much as I did," I panted as I put my clothes on.

"So," she smirked as she put her clothes on as well.

As we were coming out of the laundry room, we bumped into River. I didn't feel that we needed to speak or anything, so I scooped Natalia up so we could head to the shower together. After the shower, or round two of sex with my wife, I spent some time with my son and daughter. Once it was dinnertime, I got dressed to leave the house.

Tonight my boys and I were just gonna hang out at the club. It's been awhile since we just went out and had fun, and shit, we deserved it. I was only twenty-two years old, so the club still called my name every now and then. I threw on a white t-shirt, a navy blue windbreaker, dark jeans, and some navy blue and white Jordan 12's. I decided to go hatless since my hair was freshly cut. After spraying on my Clive Christian cologne and adding my watch and chain, I headed out.

When Dash, Leese, Rashad and I walked in, the place was packed. The music was super loud, and people were dancing extra hard. We opted out of going to my club, because I didn't feel like being a boss man tonight. I wanted to be a regular patron. We hurried to VIP because I hated to be in the mix of all these muthafuckas. I hated to be touched with someone's sweaty ass shoulder or back. When we got to the balcony VIP area, there were bottles and carafes of juice waiting, along with a couple scantily clad waitresses with flirty smiles on their faces.

"Welcome," the blond haired one cheesed.

I simply half-smiled and sat down on the plush couch. Leese and Dash on the other hand, were grinning all in her face as well. I looked over at my brother, and was happy to see him smiling and bobbing his head to the music. Now that Lucy was home with him, he seemed to be much happier.

"I see you ain't acting all glum anymore," I leaned over to him.

"Yeah, things are starting to look up I guess," he smirked and I nodded.

A couple of chicken heads were trying to get in our area, and even though I didn't want them to, Dash and Leese waved them in. I had to give it to these hoes, because their bodies were ridiculous. Rashad and I must've been thinking the same thing because we both shook our heads and raised both brows as the ladies sauntered by.

"I'm a changed man," was all I said and we both started laughing.

While sipping my drink, I looked through the bottom of the glass to see some burly ass nigga with braids coming up the stairs. I would bet my life that he just got out of jail; or maybe he broke out. This nigga reminded me of Deebo from the movie Friday. He wasn't fresh at all, but something about him said he had money. I kept my eye on him because he looked like he was coming towards us.

"He wants to come in," the lady who was working our VIP whispered into my ear over the music.

"It's straight," I replied and she switched hard as fuck back over to him.

Mr. Deebo walked in with a mug on his face, and I hoped he didn't think he was scaring anybody. He may have been built like a doublewide door, but Julius Tate wasn't scared of no nigga. We all bled the same, so it wasn't shit to be intimated by.

"Brax Northland," he reached his hand out to me before sitting down. I refused to shake it as I sipped my drink, because I knew shit was about to get real.

"Can we help you?" Rashad frowned.

I looked over and saw Dash and Leese staring, while two chicks gave them lap dances. They were waiting for me to give the okay to blast his ass. I chuckled at how ready they were.

"Which one of you niggas is Julius?" he questioned.

"That's me nigga, what's up?" I raised a brow and scooted to the edge of the couch.

"What's up is, I came to notify you that your reign is over with playboy," he stroked his beard. I was sure it had lint and moths somewhere in it.

"That's funny. My reign won't be over anytime soon. And now that you came up in here on some bullshit, you don't even have a chance to be a part of the movement," I responded.

"A part of the movement?" he scoffed.

"Yes, a part of the movement. A chance to work for me; the King of Charleston, and newly Orangeburg," I winked.

Orangeburg, South Carolina was originally his when he was out. The areas were a little over an hour away from each other, so I'm sure he was surprised that I had both areas on lock.

"Nigga, I'm 'bout old enough to put you over my fuckin' knee!

Someone must be putting cocaine on your pacifier if you think I'm gonna be working for your ass!" he shouted over the music.

"And with all the money I'm making from your territory, I can buy all the pacifiers I want nigga! Get the fuck up out my section!" I hollered.

Brax stared at me, quickly darted his eyes to Rashad and then shot up off the couch. I stood up simultaneously just in case he wanted to get down. He mugged me once more, and then turned to leave.

"Double-stick, popsicle ass nigga!" I called after him once I saw his skinny ass ankles. "Quit skipping leg day!" I added and he flicked me off as he walked down the stairs.

"You think he's gonna be a problem?" Rashad asked once I sat down.

"Oh he's definitely gonna be a fucking problem. I ain't worried though. He'll just get taken out like the rest of these niggas who refuse to get down," I shrugged and Rashad nodded.

RASHAD TATE

"I had to Rashad, she doesn't deserve you," Paula sobbed.

"That's not your place Paula! Are you fucking crazy? Now my kid is in danger of not making it!" I shouted but quickly calmed myself to adhere to the plan. I'm sorry babe, I'm just all over the place right now, I rubbed her hair out of her face.

"It's okay. I know that hoe has you acting out of character," she replied caressing my hand.

"You're right," I fake smiled at her.

Her face was stained with tears, and her long weave was disheveled. I couldn't believe that she and I had gotten to this place. I used to think Paula was the one, but she had turned into another person. I guess it's true that love will make you do some crazy ass things.

"But, I came to talk to you about my sister-in-law. You can't be blackmailing her P," I frowned and squeezed her thigh.

"I know but I was desperate!" she cried hysterically. "No one would help me! No one understood how bad I was hurting!"

"I know. I get it. But, I need the pictures you have of her and Marlon", I said.

She pulled her iPhone from her pocket, and unlocked it. She went into her camera roll, and scrolled upward until she reached the picture.

"There, they're gone, she smiled after enlarging and deleting the three pictures."

"Where are the other ones? And don't lie to me Paula. If I find out you're being sneaky again, this will never work ma, I raised my brows to let her know I was serious."

"This is it. I was so wrapped up in getting you back, I never had them developed or copied," she wiped her cheeks with the back of her hand.

"Paula."

"Rashad, I promise this is it!" she nodded.

For some reason, after all she had done, I still didn't want to text my brother and let him know to come in. However, I wasn't about to let her drive a wedge between he and I. Natalia was his wife, and I wouldn't want someone jeopardizing her freedom if I were him either. Shit, I don't want her freedom being jeopardized as her brother-in-law. On top of her blackmailing Natalia, she had possibly killed my girl and child, which were grounds for automatic termination in my book.

"What about your computer?" I questioned.

"It may be on there because of my iCloud, but I promise nowhere else," she sniffled and smiled.

I leaned over and pecked her lips gently, because I knew it was the last time. I used to love this girl; can you blame me? I pulled my phone from my pocket to text Julius.

***Me:** At the store*

I sent him the coded text and then quickly locked my phone.

"Who are you texting?" Paula quizzed with a raised eyebrow.

"Julius, just letting him know that we're all good," I half lied and she nodded.

Right after, we heard a knock at the door and I knew this was it.

My eyes fluttered open and I stared at the ceiling. Every night I'd been dreaming about the events that had taken place just before we took Paula out. Even though she more than deserved that shit, it still bothered me. Even though she killed my fucking kid before he could even make it out, I still felt bad. I guess it was because of our history together. Before she went bat shit crazy, we had some good times.

"Good morning," Lucy walked into the bedroom looking beautiful as ever.

"Good morning sexy," I half-smiled. She shot me one back and then sat in front of her mirror to do her makeup. "What are you doing today?" I asked as I sat up on the edge of the bed.

"Nothing right now. Natalia and I are going out to Ray's Lounge later though," she responded as she put some creamy shit on her face.

"Can I take you and Lumar to lunch?" I bit my lip.

"Really?" she grinned and turned to face me.

"Yeah, I know I've been kind of distant and I want you to know it's not you. I've just never dealt with anything like this ma. I've never had a serious girlfriend who was pregnant by me and got shot and all that shit. It was a little bit much but I'm good now," I smirked and stood up.

"Well I've never been a serious girlfriend, while being pregnant and then getting shot," she half joked and we laughed.

"I know, and I'm glad we are one another's first," I nodded and so did she. "I'm gonna get dressed so we can eat and go shopping before you go out with Natalia tonight."

"Okay," she replied.

I hopped in the shower and let the hot water soothe my muscles and mind. I needed to shape the fuck up and stop acting like a bitch. There's no reason for me to be neglecting my girl and my little brother. I cleaned my body then got out to brush my teeth and get dressed.

We pulled up to the restaurant, and I got out to unbuckle Lumar. Lucy chose to go to this restaurant named Cru Cafe on Pinckney Street. I was so hungry that I didn't care what she picked at this point. Lucy walked around to my side of the car so she and Lumar could hold hands as we walked into the restaurant. She looked so pretty in a tight red summer dress that stopped a few inches above her knees. Her long dark hair was really straight and sweeping the top of her tailbone. *Damn,* I grabbed onto her freehand, and we walked into the restaurant like a family.

"What do you think about me adopting him?" I asked after the waiter set our drinks down.

"You sure you want to? Don't we need to be married for that?" she cocked her head to the right.

"Probably, but we could do that too," I smiled.

"If this is a proposal, it's not very romantic," she chuckled.

"No it's not. When I do propose though, it will be much more grand trust me," I replied as I stared into her brown eyes.

"Well, I think that would make me very happy."

"Adopting him or getting married?" I questioned.

"Both," she replied.

"I love you Ms. Ouistin," I rubbed her hand.

"I love you too," she blushed.

"And you too man," I pinched Lumar's cheek as he held tightly onto a piece of bread.

Lucy grinned from ear to ear as she watched us interact. I loved seeing her so happy, especially after all the traumatic events that she'd just experienced.

I couldn't wait to step out tonight. It'd been awhile, and I needed it. All I'd been doing lately was being a wife, taking care of my babies, being nagged by my mother, and making sure my bakery was coming together. We also wanted to celebrate Lucy making it through, so we had plenty of reasons to make tonight happen.

I stepped out of the shower, and wrapped my towel around my body. I walked into my room, and began to spread body butter all over my body while it was still damp. I stood up and stared into the mirror at my naked body. I saw my stomach was starting to grow a little, but it was still flat, thank God. I never wanted to be that pregnant bitch in the club, unless it was for good reason. As I rubbed the last of the body butter over my small breasts, I saw that River was standing in the room through the mirror.

"River!" I yelped as I grabbed my robe off the chair in my room.

"I'm sorry Natalia, I just had a question and when I walked in-"

"It's fine River, what was the question?" I panted. I really wanted to ask how long had she'd been standing there watching me.

"Oh, your mother messed on the sheets and I just wanted to know whether or not I could just drop them in the washer?" she smiled.

"Umm, where is Winnie?" I quizzed.

"She's eating lunch, should I ask her?"

"No, no. Just throw the sheets away. We don't want to keep them anyway," I replied.

"Okay, and again, I'm sorry Natalia. You have a nice shape by the way," she said.

"Girl, I'm nothing like those chicks on Instagram," I joked although I was still a little weirded out.

"But that's okay. It works for you and Julius obviously loves it. I hear you guys going at it all day," she chuckled.

"Oh my gosh! I'm sorry. That's probably uncomfortable for you," I laughed.

"No, it's actually quite entertaining," she nodded. "Well, I should let you get back to what you were doing," she added and then left the room.

***

"So how is everything with Rashad? Is he still being distant?" I asked Lucy as we sat in the VIP area of Ray's.

I'm guessing that Paula didn't tell her cousin that she and I weren't friends anymore, because he still hooked Lucy and I up. We weren't twenty-one yet, but he still had bottles and juice delivered to us. I was slightly flattered because that meant I didn't look pregnant.

"Girl, I don't know what happened to him but he switched it up. He seems to be back to normal and even a little better, she replied while sipping her orange juice and tequila.

"That's good! I'm so happy, because you deserve it," I cheesed and then polished off the cranberry juice in my glass.

"What about you? Is mom still annoying?" she questioned.

"She is extremely annoying, but I think she's getting worse," I pursed my lips.

"Really? Why do you think that? The nurse said it?" she quizzed.

"No, but she told me she used the bathroom on herself in the bed," I shook my head.

"Damn," Lucy replied.

"And speaking of that nurse, I was putting body butter on and when I looked into my mirror, I saw her behind me watching," I bucked my eyes.

"What the fuck? What did you do?" Lucy chuckled.

"I didn't do anything really; we kind of just skated over it. She said she just came to ask me a question, but why would you just stand there as I'm rubbing lotion on my stomach and breasts?" I frowned.

"I think I jinxed you," Lucy laughed.

"Why do you say that?" I furrowed my brows.

"Because, remember when I said that Lisa chick liked you? I think you finally got someone who does want you," Lucy raised a brow.

"River is not gay! She told me she broke up with her man!" I shook my head in confusion.

"Hello, there is a thing called bisexual Natalia."

"No, not River. She's straight. I know it," I said although I had no idea. I mean, she said she was just there to ask me a question.

"Okaaay, but when she knocks you out with a vase and eats your pussy while you're unconscious, don't come crying to me," Lucy joked and we both burst into laughter.

Although I was laughing, I prayed that what Lucy was saying wasn't factual. I had no problem with River being bisexual, but I did have a problem with her trying to be bisexual with me. Lord, if it wasn't one thing it was another.

I woke up and looked over to see my wife lying next to me naked. The sheet was only covering a portion of her body, leaving her breasts exposed. I removed the sheet from her body completely, and she didn't budge. An evil smirk crept across my face, as I spread her smooth legs apart gently. I licked between the slit and she jumped.

"Relax babe," I whispered and she did.

I sat her legs on my shoulders and dove back in. I was licking, sucking and slurping like it was the best thing I'd ever tasted; it *was* the best thing I'd ever tasted. She arched her back as I sucked her clit harder.

"Mmmm, ahh," she cooed as I squeezed her ass.

I lifted her a little so I could slip my tongue into her hole much easier. She began to wind her hips slowly into my mouth, while calling out my name. She came hard as fuck, and her body jerked.

"Juuuu," she cried as I pushed her legs back.

I picked my head up, and stared at her pretty, pink center. I pecked it lightly, and then dove back in. I slipped my finger into her, while I flicked my tongue over her swollen button. She rubbed her small hands across my fade, as she whimpered like a little kitten.

"Babyyy," she purred as she released into my mouth a second time.

I licked her lower lips once more, and then planted a soft kiss on it before rolling off her. I got out of bed, and then proceeded to gather my things for the shower.

"Where are you going?" she asked.

"I have to go tie up some loose ends with Bart before I leave to Indianapolis tomorrow," I replied as I walked into the bathroom within our room.

"How long will you be gone?" she questioned as she followed me.

"Just three days. You know I'm gonna talk to you the whole time," I smiled and she looked away. "Come here," I said and grabbed her face to kiss her lips.

She sucked on my bottom lip and then we wrestled using our tongues. I squeezed her plump ass then lifted her in the air. She wrapped her legs around my waist as we continued to entangle ourselves in a passionate kiss. I took her into the shower, and had her screaming my name for the second time.

After Natalia's and my shower together, I took her, Jackson, and Harmony out to breakfast. Natalia always became a little somber whenever I had to go to Indianapolis, which is why I made sure that I kept in contact with her most of the day. I called her every night as well, and we would talk for hours until we fell asleep on the phone.

I was on my way to go see Bart. I told him that I wanted to meet at his office because I knew Skylar would be at the home. I didn't have time for her thirsty ass, and I didn't want to have to murk his daughter just because she was a hoe.

"How are you Mr. Tate?" Bart smiled and leaned back in his chair.

"I'm straight, 'I'm just curious as to what you wanted to talk to me about?" I frowned.

"Right, well the shipments are all set up for the days that we discussed," he nodded and stopped like he was hesitant to continue.

"I know that ain't what you called me down here for. You could've text that," I raised a brow.

"Right, my mother is sick and I need to travel to Peru to be by her side in her final days. By saying that, you will have to communicate with my daughter, Skylar if you have any problems," he half-smiled.

"Phones work in Peru, what the fuck do I need to talk to her for?" I questioned.

"They do, but I really want to focus on my mother man. Once your mother is gone, she's gone forever," he huffed. *I know that's right*, I thought as my mind drifted to my mother, Tina.

"What about your other daughter. Umm, what's her name, Leah?"

"Leah is not into this shit. I wanted a son but luckily, I have a daughter who is willing to work in my field and handle shit when I'm gone," he chuckled.

"Your wife?" I asked.

"I'm not letting you near my wife. Look, Skylar can be very professional Julius. Ah! Here she is now," he said and pointed to his door.

Skylar walked in wearing the tightest dress I'd ever seen. She couldn't even cough too hard because that shit would rip open.

"I see my daddy has given you the great news," she said flinging her long weave over her shoulder.

"I will leave you guys to get acquainted," Bart laughed and got up to leave.

"Don't be so uptight Ju, my dad will only be gone for a month," she smiled seductively as she sat on the edge of the desk.

"I'm all about my business and my money, so I don't need you on any bullshit! Don't hit me up for anything that doesn't involve that work! If I even think you trying to throw that sour ass pussy my way, you'll be the newest topic on unsolved mysteries," I said through gritted teeth and left before she could say anything.

"And you, I know what you're trying to do and it ain't gone work," I spat to Bart as I passed him in the hallway.

"Have a good day Julius," he cackled and walked back to his office.

It seemed like whenever a nigga was trying to do right, bitches wanted to fuck that up. I couldn't understand why these hoes didn't care that I had a wife. Back in the day, I would've been succumbed to her advances, but that wasn't how I was living anymore. I would die before I gave Natalia a glimpse of the old Julius. I promised her that I wouldn't hit her, which I don't even see how I did in the first place, and, that I wouldn't cheat. Nobody was gonna make me renege on that, no matter how voluptuous or sexy they were.

"Good morning baby, you have a phone call," Winnie smiled and handed me the phone as I changed Harmony's diaper.

"Thank you Winnie," I said as I tucked the phone between my ear and shoulder. "Hello?" I said into the phone.

"Hi Nat, this is Sandra," Paula's mother replied. I bucked my eyes because I was scared of the questions she had to ask.

"O-oh hi Sandra," I slightly stammered. *Be cool Natalia,* I told myself.

"Honey, I haven't been able to get in contact with Paula for a little over a month now. I know you guys aren't friends anymore, but have you spoken with her?" she questioned.

"No, no. Paula and I haven't talked since I came back from Noblesville that time," I lied.

"Oh yeah. I guess she has run off again," she exhaled heavily.

"Again?" I repeated confused.

"Yeah, whenever she breaks up with a boyfriend she skips town for months at a time," Sandra smacked her lips.

It seemed as if God was on my side. I was happy that this was a pattern for Paula, because that meant there weren't too many red flags.

"Yeah, she and Rashad had a pretty bad breakup," I nodded as if she could see me.

"Yes, I know. Gabby misses her, but she gets used to Paula ditching her for long periods of time."

"Oh, I see. Well let me know if you hear anything. Although we aren't friends, I still hope she is okay," I said playing the concerned friend role.

"I will honey, thank you. Kiss the babies and say hello to Julius for me, okay."

"I will," I said in a low tone and then disconnected the call.

I felt bad about lying to Sandra because she was a good person. But, her daughter was obviously disturbed and deserved everything that happened to her.

I slipped into my bathing suit because I was gonna go for a swim while Winnie fed Jackson and Harmony. I kissed both of their chubby cheeks as I walked by them to the outside. I loved my babies so much, and they were the cutest little things. As I walked outside, I saw River crying into her phone. *She was always in some shit*, I said to myself.

"River?" I said as I came up behind her.

"Oh Natalia, I'm on my lunch," she half-smiled and wiped her cheek.

"No, I'm just making sure you're okay," I shook my head.

"Yes, yes I'm fine. You look beautiful by the way," she chuckled, as she looked me up and down in my bathing suit.

"Thanks I guess. It's just a bathing suit," I shrugged and moved back a little.

"Yeah but it fits you so well. I wish I had a body like yours," she huffed.

"Like mine? I wish I had a body like Amber Rose," I joked.

"No, like I said, yours is perfect. You have just enough of everything. Julius is lucky," she said as she looked up into my eyes. *Maybe she is gay!* I thought.

"Yeah, I'm lucky too," I responded.

"I didn't wanna say anything, but he is very sexy!" she laughed and so did I. *Maybe she isn't gay,* my mind switched gears.

"Don't be looking at my man!" I half joked. "But are you sure you're okay?" I quizzed.

"Yeah, I think I'm just feeling down. All I do is work, and then go home and cry about Cameron," she exhaled.

"Cameron?"

"Oh I'm sorry, that's my ex-boyfriend I told you about," she nodded and smiled.

"Right umm, Lucy and I are going to Julius' club tonight, do you wanna come?" I offered because I felt bad for her.

"Are you sure? I wouldn't want to add myself to something I wasn't invited to," she replied.

"I just invited you so you're not adding yourself to anything."

"Then I would love to go. What time should I come back here? I have to leave once I'm done with your mother to get dressed," she folded her arms.

"Around 9pm is good."

"Alright, can't wait," she squealed and then rushed back inside to tend to my mother.

I swam for about thirty minutes and then decided to lay out with a glass of iced tea that Winnie had just made. As I was lying there, I felt a pair of eyes on me. I tried to ignore it, but I finally looked over to see River. She was carrying something, walking by the sliding doors. She glanced at me once more and then winked before walking away. *You're just paranoid Natalia*, I told myself. As I got up to go inside and take a bath, my phone buzzed.

Husband: Hey, just letting you know I'm still alive. I will be back tomorrow, but I need some pictures of you in the shower.

Me: Okay lol. I miss you.

Husband: I miss you too, and don't forget the money shots.

Me: Stop calling my vagina the money shot. Lol

Husband: That's what it is baby. I love you.

Me: I love you too.

Julius made it no secret that he used my pictures to jack off, and then he would delete them. I almost wished he didn't so he could use the same pictures. I was more than happy to send them though, because it was better than him running up in some hoe while he was away.

I took my bath and made sure to take some good pictures for my baby. I decided to put body butter on inside the bathroom, even though River had gone home to get dressed. Maybe I just didn't know her well enough. Some people had weird personalities, and maybe she was one of them.

I decided on a simple red Roberto Cavalli dress that hugged my small frame, and matching red stilettos. My hair was freshly pressed, and my mink acrylic nails were fresh too. I put on my jewelry then sprayed my Marc Jacobs Decadence perfume before leaving my room to kiss and tuck in my babies. When I came downstairs, Winnie let me know River was in the den waiting. I went to kiss my sleeping mother, and then walked to the den.

"Wow Natalia," River said in a low tone, as her eyes roamed my physique.

"You look nice too," I chuckled.

She had on a black tube dress with black thigh high boots. Her short curly hair was hanging down, and she appeared to have on little to no makeup.

"Thank you," she blushed.

We headed out, and went to pick up Lucy. When we pulled up to Club Rissani, it was packed as usual with a line around the damn corner. One thing about this club though, you rarely saw someone that wasn't dressed to the nines. You had your sprinkle of hood rats, but not many.

"Look at this line! My feet already hurt!" River exclaimed.

"Girl, we don't wait in line anywhere. You know who you're with?" Lucy joked and we all laughed.

As soon as we got in, the three of us were escorted to the VIP area overlooking the whole club. Lucy and River immediately started making themselves a drink, as I sipped on the guava juice they'd brought us.

"Trap Luv" by Fetty Wap came through the speakers and everyone really started to show out. Lucy stood up with her drink in her hand,

and began to sway her body. She had on a white two-piece skirt and top set, and her hair was in a long ponytail. I hopped up to join her, it felt good to be in our own space and not have guys trying to push up on us. Lucy started to twerk her ass on me jokingly, and I was laughing so hard I almost spilled my juice. I loved going out with her. Suddenly, I felt some hands touch my waist, and I looked over my shoulder to see River. I kept dancing so it wouldn't be awkward, but it definitely was. She pulled my body closer to hers as the song switched. Lucy bucked her eyes at me but I tried to ignore her. River then began to rub her hands up my body, so I pulled away and sat down.

"I'm tired," I lied.

What in the hell was she trying to do? She wasn't dancing with me like a friend would. She was dancing with me like she wanted to fuck me. I didn't know what her problem was, but she and I were not going down that road together.

"That was fun," she smirked and plopped down next to me on the club couch, as Lucy shook her head.

JULIUS

A COUPLE DAYS LATER

Now that I had a jet, I could come home at any time of the night or day that I wanted. I just had to let my pilot know two hours in advance. I'd been in Indianapolis handling a lot of shit and making sure everything was running like a well-oiled machine. I loved all the money I was getting, but the only downside was that I missed my wife.

It was 1am when I walked into the house, so I hoped Natalia was up. She was used to talking to me on the phone until two and three in the morning, so she should be wide-awake. I walked into the bedroom, and she was watching a movie on Netflix.

"Julius," she whispered and sat up in the bed. The room was dark, but you could still see how beautiful she was.

"Hey baby," I smiled and handed her the yellow roses I'd gotten for her.

"Thank you!" she beamed and then turned on the lamp on the nightstand.

"How has everything been going?" I asked as I undressed down to my wife beater and boxers.

"It's umm, it's okay. I wanna talk to you about River," she replied.

"What's up?" I asked as I cut the lamp off and walked to my side of the bed.

"I think she wants to have sex."

"With who? You?" I laughed.

"Julius, that's not funny! I'm serious!" she pouted.

"Natalia relax. I'm sure you're just paranoid," I chuckled.

"She always compliments my body," she said.

"Well, can you blame her? It is pretty nice." I started to kiss her neck, and pull down the straps of her gown.

"Juliuuuss. Listen to me," she whined as I took her small round breasts into my hands and licked her nipples.

"Go ahead and talk, I'm all ears," I said in between licks and sucks.

"Mmmm, s-she, you need to-" she stuttered, and then I lifted my head to slip my tongue into her mouth.

I tongued her down for a little bit, and then sat up to remove my shirt. I smiled down at her as she eyed my chest.

"When did you get that?" she pointed to her name tatted on my chest.

"Couple days ago while I was in Naptown." I bit my lip as a beautiful smile spread across her face.

"About time, I been had your name on me," she replied.

"I know. You've always been all about me, I'm just playing catch up," I said in a low tone as I lowered my body on top of hers.

"I love you," she whispered and pecked my lips.

"I love you more girl," I looked into her eyes.

"I don't think that's possible."

I dipped my tongue into her mouth, and slid into her warm, tight, wet walls.

"So are we gonna go get at these niggas or what?" my homeboy Leese asked. This nigga was always willing to shoot first and ask questions later.

"Yeah, do you know how many it is?" I inquired.

"About six dudes, is what Jabari told me," Dash replied.

That nigga Brax had his little niggas trying to sell on my turf and obviously, it didn't sit well with me. I wasn't hesitant to put a hot one in his workers, because they should've known that what they were doing was a no-go. That had been my area for the longest now and I wasn't letting anybody work on it.

"They not even really pushing nothin' because their product ain't as good as yours," Leese shook his head and Dash chuckled.

"It's the principle though. I ain't worried about these niggas having better shit. They need to learn to respect me. Brax needs to realize that I'm the king of this city and that ain't gone fucking change."

"So what's the plan?" Rashad asked.

"This shit ain't nothing for the big dogs like us to do. Hit up Jabari and Luke to let them know to take them niggas out. Then we will wait and see how Brax reacts. If he doesn't get the hint by then, it will be time to just take the nigga out," I replied and everyone nodded.

"I'm gone call Jabari right now," Dash said as he pulled out his phone.

I was really trying to give Brax's ass the benefit of the doubt, but he was really testing me. He would soon find out that it was nothing for me to take his ass out though.

As I was driving towards my house to pick up my family for dinner, my work phone rang. Bart's office number showed up on the display screen of my radio. I rolled my eyes and then tapped the answer button.

"What?" I spat.

"I was just checking on you to make sure everything went well on your Indianapolis visit," Skylar cooed into the phone.

"Why? You have nothing to do with my operation in Indiana," I replied.

"I know but I wanted to see if you needed anything from this side of things," she said.

"What the fuck is you talking about?" I frowned even though she wasn't in my presence.

"Your other connect is keeping up with the shipments you need for Indianapolis? Because if not, I can see-"

"My other connect is not any of your business. I told you not to fucking call me unless it had something to do with what I got going on with Bart. Stop trying to think of shit to say just to call me," I shook my head as I made a left turn.

"I'm not making up stuff to call you about, don't flatter yourself," she scoffed.

"Yeah you are and it is very obvious. Get a life," I spat and hung up the phone.

I really wasn't trying to bump her off, especially since she hadn't done anything to me really. However, as soon as her little hoe ass antics started to spill over into my marriage, she was a goner. I didn't give a fuck whose daughter she was.

NATALIA

THREE WEEKS LATER

River had been kind of normal for the past few weeks and I was starting to relax more around her. After that little club stint, I was distant as hell, so maybe that's what did it.

"How are you feeling Dalia?" I asked my mother as I entered her room. River had just gone home for the day and I was ecstatic.

My mother was looking worse every time I saw her. The doctor told me that her cancer was spreading fast because she took forever to have her symptoms examined. There were things going on with her body over a year ago, but she was too scared to go have it checked out, fearing the worse. Unfortunately, that did much more harm to her. The only reason she finally decided to go to the doctor was because the pelvic pain she usually had become so unbearable that she couldn't even walk.

"Look at my hair," she replied as a tear ran down her smooth brown cheek. She held up her once thick locks in her hand.

"You're still beautiful," I half-smiled and wiped the tear from her face.

"Don't lie! Appreciate your beauty while you still have it," she sniffled.

"Dal-"

"Leave Natalia, I'm sleepy," she cut in.

I kissed her cheek and then hurried outside. I loved my mother even though she always treated me like a nuisance. I prayed every night hoping that she would make it, but it didn't look good at all.

After failing at making my mom feel better, I dressed Jackson and Harmony so that they could get some fresh air. I was gonna go to the grocery store because tonight Julius was coming home from Indiana. He'd already let me know he would be here by 10pm, so I wanted to have a nice dinner waiting for him. Winnie had already cooked for the rest of us but being pregnant, I could eat one hundred times a day.

As we were walking past the baked goods section, Jackson started to point to a case of cupcakes. I started to push past them and he burst into tears.

"Mommy can make those for you baby," I wipe his tears and kissed his fat cheek.

"Noooo," he sobbed. That was all he knew how to say.

"Jackson, stop it baby," I pleaded. He just stared at me and poked his little lip out as Harmony played with her toy keys.

"Fine you little brat, but when my bakery opens you won't even like these," I joked as I sat the set of four cupcakes in his little lap. He didn't even want to eat them, he just held them in his chunky hands.

"Excuse me, did I hear you say you had a bakery?" some huge guy asked. He had to be a bouncer for a club.

"Yes, well we don't open until next week. I'm gonna have a grand opening," I smiled.

"I see. I'm very well known in the food industry, and if you'd like, I could have some food critics come through and give you a review," he offered.

"Wow really? That would be great," I grinned.

"It would. And by the way that you just talked about your cupcakes, I would love to come to the grand opening myself."

"Yeah, sure, of course. I'm Natalia by the way," I reached my hand out to shake.

"Very beautiful. I'm Braxton," he replied and smirked.

"Nice to meet you Braxton. Do you have a card or something that I could take, or an email I could write down?" I asked.

"Of course, why don't we exchange emails?" he said as he reached into his suit jacket pocket.

"Mine is *Tate.Natalia@HarmonyBakeShoppe.com*," I read off to him and he wrote it down.

"All my information is on there," he responded as he handed me a fresh business card.

"Well it was nice meeting you and I look forward to speaking with you."

"Likewise, I just wish you were available," he bit his lip and gestured towards my ring.

"You're three years too late," I joked as I wiped Jackson's face.

"I see that. Have a nice evening Natalia," he winked and then walked away.

It's crazy where you'll find opportunities. I knew having food critics taste and review my cupcakes would be good publicity. I also knew if they hated them, it would be bad. I had faith in my skills though and I'd never had one single complaint in the past, so I wasn't too worried.

"That dinner was good, but I'm still hungry," Julius said as he carried me upstairs to the bedroom.

He laid me down on the bed in my all white lingerie and stared into my eyes as he removed his shirt. His smooth caramel complexion was so perfect that it made my mouth water. His abs were perfectly chiseled and his strong arms had my body begging to be held. I loved seeing my name tatted on his chest, it turned me on to know he was finally all mine.

He brought his hands to my lace thong and started to remove them, but I stopped him. I pushed him up so that he was standing and then pushed his sweats and boxers down. After he stepped out of them, I took his long thick dick into my mouth. I teased the tip like he liked me to, while I massaged his balls. I slid him into my wet mouth inch by inch, while enjoying the sounds of his soft moans.

"Deep throat that shit Nat," he panted as I took him fully into my mouth.

I bobbed my head up and down on his dick, while letting my spit do its own thing. He placed his hand on the back of my head, and rotated his hips into my mouth. I took every stroke like the pro I had become.

"I'm about to nut. Fuck," Julius grunted.

"Give it to me daddy," I purred and before I could finish getting the sentence out, he spilled his seeds into my mouth. I swallowed it up like it was medicine.

"I love your freaky ass," he exhaled heavily as he unhooked my bra.

He dropped down to suck my hard nipples, while playing with my clit through my panties. He kept his mouth latched onto my nipple as he tugged my panties down.

"Sit on my face," he said in a low tone, as he laid down on the bed. "Keep those heels on," he added once he saw me about to undo the strap.

I smiled and shook my head then mounted his face.

"Let's do it backwards," he smirked.

"You're so nasty," I replied and got up to turn around.

As soon as my pussy got close to his mouth, he started to suck on my clit. He squeezed my ass and smacked it, as he made love to me with his mouth.

"Fuck Juuu," I whimpered.

"Stop it," he mumbled referring to me trying to suck his dick.

I stopped and then ground my hips slowly, giving him unlimited access to my pussy. He spread my cheeks, and then licked from my clit all the way to my anal cavity.

"Oooh," I shivered as I bit my lip. "Ugghhhh," I cried out immediately after, as I felt myself releasing.

He pulled me closer by my waist, and attacked my pussy again as if he couldn't get enough. He held my ass cheeks open as he licked and sucked everywhere. Electric waves shot throughout my body as he sucked the life out of me. I felt another orgasm rising, and my body was starting to tense up. I planted my palms onto the bed, and pushed my pussy into his mouth while he plunged his fingers in and out of me.

"Juu, I'm cumming daddy," I whimpered. Right after I said it, I came all over his mouth and fingers. My body jerked violently as I pulled my clit out of his mouth.

I laid on my back and he kissed my stomach a couple times while I rubbed his head.

"You're starting to show a little," he smiled up at me.

"I know," I half-smiled.

He kissed my stomach one more time, for a little bit longer, and then trailed kisses up to my neck. He dipped his tongue into my mouth and then wiggled his way inside me. He moved slowly, giving me time to adjust to his length and girth.

"You're so wet Nat," he whispered into my mouth. "I love this pussy," he added while biting my bottom lip.

He pinned my hands behind my head, and rotated his hips as he thrust into me. I was so wet that I could feel it dripping down onto the sheets. Every pump he delivered made my legs shake from the pleasure. He sucked and kissed my neck, and I closed my eyes to enjoy every way he touched me. He lifted his head, and began to tongue me down again.

"I love you Julius," I moaned in between kisses.

He played with my nipples, and then sped up his pace making a tear slip out of my eye. He licked my tear, and then pinned my hands back above my head again.

"I love you too Nat," he finally replied.

"Mmmmm," we both grunted softly as we came together.

For some reason this sex session seemed to be more of a spiritual connection than a physical one. I felt like we were one, and it made it all the better. We laid there in one another's embrace, and kissed for what seemed like forever.

JULIUS

Natalia and I had been really busy with work, so I wanted to take her shopping and to lunch. We usually always brought the kids with us, but I wanted to have some time alone outside of the bedroom.

We decided to go to the Tanger Outlet Center in North Charleston, because they had a wide variety of shops. I already knew that Natalia was gonna go ham in these places because it was rare that we came here.

"You like this one?" Natalia asked as she lifted a dress in the air. We'd been in BCBGMAXAZRIA for the last forty-five minutes and I was already ready to go. This was the tenth store we visited.

"Don't you have that dress already?" I frowned.

"Yes, but it's pale pink. This one is tan," she replied. What the fuck was the difference?

"Right, well yeah, I like it babe. I like anything on you," I smiled and she blushed. Thank God, she headed towards the register so we could pay and leave.

"We have to get some things for Jackson and Harmony. Then we have to go to SAKS, and then we can go," she said as we walked out the store as if that was gonna make me feel better.

"Anything for you baby," I said dryly as I watched her little plump ass in her skinny jeans. I was gone wear that pussy out tonight after all this shit.

We shopped for our kids in Janie and Jack's for about an hour, and then it was finally time to make the last stop at SAKS. We weren't in there five minutes, and I heard a loud familiar voice coming in. I looked up and saw Skylar, Bart's daughter. I hoped that this was just a coincidence, but something told me that she was taking her thirstiness to a whole new level.

"Julius?" she called out once she saw me, and Natalia immediately looked her way.

"What's up?" I replied nonchalantly.

"What are you doing here?" Skylar grinned.

"Spending time with my wife," I turned my lip up because she was already pissing me off.

"Julius, who is this?" Natalia raised a brow.

"This is Skylar, Bart's daughter. You met her at the Orangeburg celebration baby," I replied.

"Yes, nice to see you again Natalia," Skylar nodded and shifted her weight from her left to her right hip. "You know, your husband and I are working together now. He's a real hard worker," she added and bit her lip.

"Oh is he?" Natalia chuckled.

"Yeah he is. Well enjoy the rest of your day you two," Skylar cheesed and then turned on her heels to switch out of the store. She ain't even buy shit, which let me know this was planned.

"I'm ready to go," Natalia said.

"You didn't even get anything babe," I frowned.

"I didn't see anything I liked," she spat and then walked towards the door.

I quickly hopped up and followed her, while trying to keep a hold onto all of her shopping bags. I didn't catch her until we reached the car. I unlocked it with the remote, and she got in and slammed the door as I loaded up the trunk. Skylar was gonna get an earful.

"Baby what's wrong with you?" I questioned when I got into the car.

"What did she mean when she said you were a hard worker?" she asked as a single tear ran down her face.

"Wait, you think I'm fucking her?"

"Are you? It wouldn't be the first time you've cheated on me," she sniffled.

"Natalia, I have not been cheating on you, ma. I've been all about you, and you know that," I said in a low tone.

She didn't say anything. She just stared straight ahead, as more tears started to produce. She quickly wiped them but it didn't help much. I leaned over and stared into her face for a couple seconds before speaking.

"Natalia Lillian Tate, I love you and I have been faithful to you. I promise," I whispered. "To be perfectly honest, she *has* been pushing up on me, but I've been declining her advances the whole time."

"You can't cheat on me anymore Julius, you have to be good to me! I've given you too many chances!" she sobbed.

"If anybody knows that I do baby. I swear on my life that I've been faithful aight. Don't let that girl get in your head, that's what she wants," I said in a low tone and then planted a soft kiss on her lips.

At first, she didn't reciprocate it, but she finally parted her lips and let me kiss her passionately like I wanted to. After kissing so hard and so long to the point where we ran out of breath, I pulled away. I wiped her pretty face and then pecked her once more.

"You straight?" I smiled.

"Yeah," she chuckled.

"Good, stop crying. You're way too pretty to be crying over a nigga, even if it is me," I told her as I fastened my seatbelt and prepared to back out of my parking space. "You still want to go eat?" I questioned.

"Of course," she cheesed. Thank God.

I dropped my wife off after we had lunch, and immediately went over to Bart's house. Hopefully, that bitch was there. I didn't want to call first, because I wanted to do a surprise pop up like she had done on me. I pulled up to the house and was happy to see her little Mercedes truck parked in the driveway.

"Seeing me once today wasn't enough?" Skylar answered the door.

I snatched her up by the neck, and backed her into the house. It'd been a long ass time since I had put my hands on a woman, but this right here was a bitch. I kicked the front door closed and then banged her into the wall.

"You thought I was fucking playing?" I said through gritted teeth as I watched her gasp for air. "Well I'm not! Don't fuck with me Skylar, I don't give a fuck who your damn daddy is!" I shouted in her face then released my grip around her neck.

"Are you out of your fucking mind?" she screamed as she panted. "How dare you come in here and put your hands on me nigga!"

"You lucky I ain't light yo' hoe ass up!" I hollered.

"Fuck you Julius! I'm the wrong bitch to fuck with!"

"And I'm most definitely the wrong nigga, so I guess we will just have to see what happens! But, I will tell you this, you have one more time to pull some desert thirsty ass stunt like you did today! Fuck with me and Bart will be burying more than his mother," I grimaced.

One more time! One more fucking time and I was deadin' that bitch! I put that on my dead mother's grave that I would be putting a hollow tip in that bitch if she came incorrect again!

HARMONY'S BAKE SHOPPE GRAND OPENING

This evening marked the grand opening of my bakery, and I was nervous *and* excited. I knew my cupcakes were great, but I was still a little scared of what the critics would say. Braxton emailed me the details letting me know the critic's names. Lucy and I looked them up on Google, just to make sure they were legit and they definitely were. I didn't expect them to be so well known, but I was happy they were nonetheless.

"Casey, Nikki and Brittani, here are your hats and aprons," I told the three ladies I hired to work the front of the store.

They were all older than I was so it was kind of weird that I was their boss. Julius said it didn't matter though, and to make sure that they respected me regardless. Our age difference was only three to four years so it wasn't too bad I guess.

"Okay, so remember the promotion ladies. If they buy three cupcakes, they get two free," I said and they nodded excitedly. "Savory cupcakes are not included," I added.

"And don't forget to give them the punch cards so that they will be more likely to come back," Lucy told them and I nodded in agreement.

"They'll come back anyways, Natalia's cupcakes are bomb as hell," Nikki replied and we all laughed.

"Hey baby, congratulations," Julius entered the back room with flowers. He leaned down to kiss me and rubbed my small baby bump.

"Thank you honey," I said as I handed them to Lucy to put in water. "Where is River? She said she would help tend to the critics whenever I was busy," I said walking from the back. Just as I came to the front, I saw her coming inside.

"I almost thought you weren't coming," I exhaled.

"I would never break a promise I made to you," she responded.

"So they will be sitting at those tables over there. Make sure that no customers sit there okay?" I said ignoring her weird statement.

"Got it boss. You look gorgeous by the way," she commented and then walked to the back to put her stuff down. I shook my head and followed her to go check on the bakers.

It was 5pm and the opening was in full swing. We were extremely busy and even started to run out of multiple flavors. The critics loved all of the cupcakes I gave them so far and the nervousness I had finally started to die down.

"The lady that hooked you up with the food critics is coming?" Julius asked as he stuck his fork into one of my pecan pie cupcakes.

"It's a guy, and he's not here yet," I replied as I searched the busy store with my eyes. "Oh there he is," I pointed and stood up.

Julius froze as he and the guy made eye contact. A smile spread across Braxton's face as Julius shot daggers at him.

"Thanks for coming!" I beamed once I neared Braxton.

"No problem beautiful," he half-smiled and gave me a hug.

"Would you like a couple of complimentary cupcakes?" I offered.

"Absolutely," he replied as he eyed me from head to toe.

"Just go to the side and let Casey know. You can have two cupcakes on me," I said as I gestured for him to walk over.

I walked slowly and carefully through the crowd of people so that I could make it back to Julius. I couldn't help but notice he had an angry expression and kept looking over at Braxton.

"Are you okay Ju?" I quizzed.

"How did you meet that nigga?" he gritted.

"We ran into each other at the grocery store."

"After tonight, you need to cease all contact with him," Julius spat.

"What? Why, he really helped me-"

"Cut it off Natalia! Don't ask me anything else about it," he glared at me and I just nodded because I was caught off guard by his sudden outburst.

Besides, that little tiff between Julius and I, the night was a hit. The critics loved my cupcakes and promised me a great review on their blogs. The store made $4000 tonight, which was much more than I expected. If we could make that daily, I would be able to open up another location without asking Julius to put up for it.

Once the last few people left, I went to the back to look for my girls, bakers, and then Lucy and River. I thanked them and said my goodbyes to my team, and then went in search of my friends.

"Thank you so much Lucy," I grinned as I walked into my office.

"No problem. When you get famous, you better make sure you mention me!" she half joked as she picked up her purse.

"You know I will. Where is River?" I asked.

"Bathroom. See you later best friend," she hugged and kissed me then switched out.

"Great job tonight Natalia," River smirked as she walked into my office.

"Thank you and thanks for helping out today," I replied.

"I'd do anything for you," she said. That was it; I had to say something.

"River, are you- do you like me?" I inquired.

"Of course I like you," she giggled.

"No like me as in, you have romantic feelings for me," I reiterated.

"Umm, no. You're nice and all but I don't swing that way," she shook her head and folded her arms.

"I was just asking because of the things you say," I chuckled nervously because I was slightly embarrassed now.

"Just because I compliment you, doesn't mean I want you Natalia. Not everyone is interested in you," she scoffed.

"I don't think everyone is interested in me, I was just wondering. I'm sorry River, I guess I was just paranoid," I replied.

"It's cool. See you tomorrow morning," she exhaled and then left.

I wanted to smack myself because I felt so stupid. She probably thought I was some conceited little bitch that assumed everyone wanted a piece. I wasn't like that at all though, I just genuinely thought she wanted more from me than a friendship.

I locked the place up, and turned on the alarm before leaving. As I drove home, I thought about the way Julius acted tonight. He and Braxton didn't speak to one another all night, but I did see them glaring at each other every now and then. I was relieved when Braxton finally decided to leave. I pulled up to my home, and took a deep breath before entering the house to confront Julius.

"How much did you make?" Julius asked as I walked into the bedroom. He was sitting on the bed watching Harlem Nights.

"A lot," I responded dryly as I began to undress.

He watched me undress and change into my nightgown. I dimmed the lights in our bedroom, and then walked to my side of the bed without uttering another word. I propped the pillow up behind me to support my back, and stared at Eddie Murphy and Jasmine Guy.

"Your back hurts?" Julius asked. I shook my head yes without looking his way.

"Come here and let me give you a massage," he offered.

"I'm fine," I said as I slid down, and laid on my side with my back to him.

"Don't be mad baby," he whispered as he hugged me from behind, while caressing my small belly. "I didn't mean to yell at you, I just can't have you associating with him," he added and kissed the nape of my neck.

I didn't say anything back and just shifted my body. He craned his neck around and pecked my lips. I pretended to be sleep, so he turned me on my back.

"Stop Julius, I'm tired," I whined.

"So what. I'm not letting you go to bed angry," he smiled as he kissed my face and then my neck.

"I'm not angry," I chuckled because his neck kisses tickled.

"Then tell me you love me," he picked his head up, and stared down into my face.

"You know I love you."

"Not good enough," he said and went back to attacking my neck. I felt like I was gonna pee because it tickled so much.

"Okay! Okay!" I laughed. "I love you, daddy," I said seductively.

"That's better," he smirked and then dipped his tongue into my mouth.

JULIUS

Brax had me hot as fuck trying to mess with my family. I had no idea what his intentions were with Natalia, but I wasn't gonna wait to find out. Fucking with me is one thing but coming for my wife or kids was a whole 'nother thing.

I saw him walking out of Target, and quickly got out of my car. It was around 12pm on a Tuesday, so there weren't that many cars in the parking lot. As he neared his car, he spotted me and chuckled to himself.

"How you doing Julius?" he smiled.

"What the fuck you trying to get cozy with my wife for nigga?" I frowned.

"Look, I was just helping her out. It was all innocent," he cackled with his big ass.

"Well make that the last fucking time you do anything nice for my woman," I spat.

"Nah, you ain't about to push up on me barking orders and shit lil' nigga!" he growled.

"I'm warning you homie. You've been really working my nerves. You don't wanna end up like ya little homies you sent to work my block," I threatened.

"Oh yeah, I ain't forgot about that. Watch your back," he cheesed with his weird ass.

"For some reason, I doubt I need to," I winked and booked it back to my car. When I got in, he was still standing there with a dumb ass look on his face.

This nigga was playing games as if I knew nothing about him. Did he really think I was that dumb? Hey, maybe it would continue to work to my advantage if he thought I was just come young dumb nigga.

Brax has a whole little family at home. He lives with his baby mama; this chick named Sonia. Sonia was sexy as fuck and bourgeois as fuck too. She acted as if her nigga was still the king, always keeping her nose in the air. She had a light honey complexion and was thick in all the right places. Every nigga besides my team and myself, have tried to get at her while Brax was in jail and she swatted every one of them off like flies. Those niggas weren't Julius Tate though. Sonia had plenty of reasons to have her nose in the air, but Brax still being king wasn't one of them.

At first, I was slightly worried, because I couldn't pursue her like I needed to since I was married. I wanted to take a picture of her sucking my dick and send it to Brax in the mail. But, because I was a married man, that couldn't go down. Even though it would be for a somewhat good cause, I refused to cheat on Natalia. Although it was a slim chance that she'd find out, I didn't want to do her like that. I was just gonna spring a little harmless flirting on Sonia's ass and lure her to one of the homies.

Plenty of times in the past, way before Natalia, shit way before Bianca, I used to have bitches so in love with me that they would agree to fuck my homeboys. Y'all thought I was bad when Natalia met me. That was nothing compared to how I was a couple years before her. They thought they were just being down for me, but they should've realized that any man that would ask you or even let you fuck his boys don't give two shits about you. I don't even think I would be able to function if another nigga fucked Natalia, let alone one of my friends.

I pulled up to the Starbucks on King Street because Alonzo let me know she stopped there every day on her lunch break. Sonia was a schoolteacher, so she was nothing like these little hood rats that usually dated drug dealers. Anyway, there was a park right in front of Freddo's, which was next door to Starbucks. I pulled up, shut my engine off, slipped off my wedding band and then hopped out. I wasn't dressed too fancy because honestly, that wasn't my style. I wore a white t-shirt, a black Balmain jacket, black jeans, Supreme Jordan 5's and an Andre Emery snapback.

I walked into the place and just my luck, she was the last person standing in line. I came up behind her and pretended that I was gonna order something like a regular customer. She was whining into the phone about something and I was sure she was talking to her bitch ass baby daddy. There were two people on the register at the front, so we were both able to come up and order at the same time.

"An iced tall hazelnut latte please," she told her barista. I saw her look over at me out the corner of my eye, as she continued to talk into the phone.

"What is that strawberry thing you guys have?" I quizzed as if I really wanted to know.

"Oh well, it could either be the strawberry Frappuccino or the smoothie," my barista replied.

"I see, what do you suggest?" I looked over at Sonia.

"Well, do you like thicker drinks?" she smiled and it was very seductive.

I was slightly caught off guard because she wasn't coming off as the bourgeois bitch I'd heard about. She seemed like she was ready and willing to get dicked down by another nigga.

"I like all drinks," I responded.

"Go with the Frappuccino, more flavor," she winked and then grabbed her receipt from the young barista.

I ordered my drink in the smallest size because I hadn't planned to really drink it. I walked to the area where you pick it up and made sure to stand very close to Ms. Sonia. She finished her conversation, and looked over to me as she hung up.

"I'm Sonia," she stuck her hand out. She was wearing a tight ass pants suit that hugged every part of her curvy body.

"Ju," I told her not wanting to give my full name just yet.

"Ju? That's interesting. So I guess you're picking this drink up for your girl?" she raised a brow. Wow, she was using a nigga's line. Dudes always said shit like that to see if you were taken or not.

"I don't have a girl," I replied and cringed on the inside. *This ain't cheating, it's all a part of a plan Julius*, I told myself.

"What? Good looking guy like you?" she moved closer to me.

"Hey, sometimes you can't find the right one," I shrugged.

"I see," she chuckled and then grabbed her drink, which appeared on the bar. "Well, what are you looking for that you can't seem to find?" she inquired.

"I'm just looking for someone that's down for me. Down to do whatever, and whenever," I said in a low tone and I could tell she was feeling some type away.

"Not too much to ask I guess," she exhaled. "I would love to give you my number," she half-smiled.

She must've seen dollar signs because this was way too easy. Or, maybe she was doing this for her baby daddy. Whatever the reason was, I was smarter than they both were.

"I'll take that," I said as I pulled out my work phone.

"Aren't you gonna call me so I can store yours?" she frowned as I walked to grab my drink.

"No, I'll hit you when I need you, ma. Just be ready," I winked and sipped my drink. To my surprise, the shit was bomb as fuck and I downed it during the ride home.

Once I pulled into my driveway, I put my wedding band back on, and then called my brother so I could update him on this bitch. The only reason she was dodging these other niggas was because she didn't think they had any coins. She was more than willing to throw that pussy my way because she knew I had money. She didn't trip off me giving her my nickname because her groupie ass already knew who I was. I smiled at that because it was gonna be much easier now that I knew she was just like the rest of these money hungry hoes out here.

"What up bro?" my brother smiled into the phone. What was he so happy about?

"Man, Sonia is gonna be easier than Easy Mac nigga," I joked and he laughed.

"Word? I thought she was all uppity," he said.

"Me too man, but she pushed up on me way more than I did her," I chuckled.

"Hmm, maybe Brax told her to come for you if she met you."

"Maybe he did, but I'm one hundred steps ahead of the both of their asses already. That bitch about to be my slave," I nodded.

"How you gonna do that without giving her no dick?" he questioned.

"Easy, I'll figure something out. In the meantime, we just need to make sure he isn't selling on our blocks. I'm giving him one more chance to shape up and if he doesn't we taking him out."

"I feel you," Rashad replied.

I was tired of making threats. No more threats would be made from now on, not with Brax nor Skylar. The next thing that pops off, I'm killing one of them.

ONE MONTH LATER

I made my mother some lunch this afternoon, but she barely ate any of it. She was becoming so skinny, and for some reason, I felt that I could fatten her up by feeding her. She never really said much anymore and I was surprisingly missing her unkind words.

River was doing a great job with her though. I was worried that maybe she was the reason my mother was deteriorating, but the doctor she goes to said otherwise. He told me River was actually doing the opposite to my mother's condition. She may have been far worse off without her he said. Besides doing her job correctly, she wasn't acting all strange and flirty like before. I felt bad about approaching her the night of my opening even more now.

"River, I'm gonna go take a little nap," I said as we walked past one another. She was coming in to check on my mother, and I was leaving.

"Alright, have a good one," she smiled and so did I.

Lately, this baby had been making me more tired. My feet and back were starting to hurt badly too. I missed getting a massage from Julius, but as usual, he was over in Indianapolis handling business. He said he'd be back in two days though and I could not wait.

I walked into Julius and my bedroom, dimmed the lights down low, and then changed into my nightgown. I wasn't a person who could sleep in my street clothes, even if it was a nap. I climbed into the bed, and fell asleep almost as soon as I hit the pillow.

I was half-asleep and I felt a sensation between my legs. I was caught off guard at first, but then a smile crept across my face. Julius was sucking gently on my clit and slurping up all my juices.

"Mmmm," I cooed with my eyes still closed.

He must've told me he wasn't gonna be home for two days so that he could surprise me. I loved when he did this.

"Juuu," I whimpered and balled the sheets into my hands.

I was still half-asleep, but I was slowly waking up. I reached my hand down to caress his head just the way he liked, but it wasn't his short curls down there, it was a head of long hair. I jumped slightly, and pinned my chin to my chest to see the person attacking my center so well. It was River. She looked up at me as she continued to feast, and pinned my wrists at my side.

"River stooopp," I whispered, trying to make my sleepy body move. She didn't stop however, and soon enough I released into her mouth. She licked me clean, and then let my wrists go as she stood up.

"What are you doing?" I frowned.

"You didn't like it?" she questioned as she wiped her mouth.

"That's not the point River, I'm married!" I spat as I sat up to look for my underwear.

"Julius won't mind. I'm not a guy," she giggled.

"I thought you said you didn't have feelings for me."

"Well, now you know that I do," she grinned.

"Get out of my room River, before I fire you! Don't ever come into my room again!" I shouted in a low tone.

"I see why Julius is so head over heels for you. You taste so good Natalia," she smirked and then walked out of my room.

I hopped off the bed then rushed to lock the door. I darted to the bathroom within my bedroom and turned on the bathwater and Jacuzzi bubbles. Did she really just come up here and eat me out? I cheated on Julius, something I'd never done nor planned to do. But then again, I didn't even know she was doing it. When I woke up, she was already down there doing her thing! And maybe River was right, she wasn't even a man, so Julius may not even care. Guys liked the thought of women pleasing each other.

I picked up the cordless phone next to the tub and quickly dialed Lucy. I knew she would tell me the best thing to do for myself.

"Hello?" she answered.

"Lucy, are you alone?" I asked.

"Yeah, Rashad went with Julius this trip," she exhaled.

"Oh okay," I said.

"Why? What's wrong?" she quizzed.

"Well River, she-she gave me oral sex," I replied and then held my breath.

"What the fuck?" Lucy burst into laughter.

"Lucy! What should I do? I wanna tell Julius."

"No Natalia! He's gonna be mad as fuck," she responded.

"What? Why? It's not like River is a guy," I complained.

"It doesn't matter Nat. Only person he wants touching you in that way is him. Now if he was there, then he wouldn't care," she chuckled.

"Yeah, I guess," I huffed and sunk down under the bubbles some more.

"Now I need some details, did she knock you unconscious like I predicted? Or did she seduce you with some Fiery Ron's barbecue?" Lucy inquired and then cackled loudly.

"I hate you," I giggled. "But no, I was taking a nap and when I woke up she was going to town. I thought it was Julius so I didn't move. Then when I reached down to touch his head, it was long hair!" I exclaimed as Lucy chuckled.

"You don't know the difference between Julius going down on you versus someone else?" she asked.

"Yeah I do. He knows my spots a little better and he usually has his strong hands on my thighs," I smiled as I reminisced.

"Freak, I told you that hoe wanted you. Was it any good?"

"Bye Lucy," I laughed and quickly disconnected.

I'm not crazy. I'm just in love. Natalia was so beautiful. From the first day I met her, I knew she and I were meant to be. At first I wasn't even gonna pursue her, but she was always flirting with me. She always told me how pretty I was, and even went as far as to tell me that I would find the one very soon. In other words, she meant that she was the one for me. I'd never even been with a girl and I knew she hadn't either, but it was something about her that reeled me in.

I was lying in my bed looking on her Instagram page. Her smile was so alluring, and her body was so perfect. She wasn't thick per say, but her small frame still had a voluptuous shape to it. I was so upset that she woke up while I was eating her out, because I hadn't even got to explore the rest of her body. As soon as I slid her panties down, I couldn't help myself, I had to taste her. Julius was a lucky guy, but he didn't deserve her. He worked too much and left her lonely a couple days out of the week. It worked in my favor though because the more he left her the closer she and I would become.

Once I was ninety-six weeks into her page, I decided to exit out of the app. I had much better footage of her that I wanted to partake in. I reached into my purse and retrieved the Flipcam that I put into her room every morning before my shift. You see, every day that I came, she would be in her mother's room. While she was, I would go set my camera up in the TV stand and then go to her mom's room to start work. I knew she was always in her mom's room in the morning because she wanted to run into me.

Anyway, I plugged my camera into my computer, and loaded on the videos. They were videos of her dressing, sleeping, and my favorite -putting lotion on. I laid back with the computer in my lap, and reached my hand down into my underwear. I toyed with my clit, as I watched Natalia spread mango body butter all over her body. She wore it every day. I loved the scent of it, and how every time she walked by or came near me it filled my nostrils.

"Oooh," I purred as I came all over my fingers from seeing her rub the lotion onto her semi-flat stomach. The baby she was carrying was starting show.

I sat and watched the rest of the video, admiring her blue under-garments against her honey colored complexion. She put her long brown hair into a braid, and then slipped into some shorts and a top. Once she left the room, I cut the recording off. This had become a routine for me. I would come home and watch the video I'd recorded, and then go to sleep dreaming about her. Tonight was no different.

ONE WEEK LATER

I arrived to the Tate residence, ready to start my shift. Taking care of Dalia was starting to bother me, because she wasn't getting any better. I could tell that she was embarrassed every time she couldn't hold her bowel movements, or when a new plug of hair would come out. I prayed for her every night, but it didn't seem to be working.

"Good morning Natalia," I smiled at my boss as I entered Dalia's room. I'd just come from placing my camera upstairs, and was ready to get to work.

"Good morning River," she half-smiled and stood to her feet.

She was wearing skinny jeans and a beige layered top. Her long hair was braided into two braids like Pocahontas. I loved her so much.

"You look beautiful today," I commented. "Doesn't she Ms. Dalia?" I asked her mother.

"She looks the same as she always does," Dalia spat. I hated when she was mean to Natalia. It was so hard watching someone berate and insult the person that you loved.

"I'm gonna go get my babies together, and then help Winnie with breakfast," Natalia exhaled and then quickly left the room.

"Why do you hate Natalia so much?" I asked Dalia.

"I don't hate her. I love her. She just annoys the shit out of me," she turned her lip up.

"But why? She's so sweet," I frowned. I was confused. How could anyone hate someone like Natalia?

"Because, she ruined my life. I thought when I got pregnant by her father that it would solidify us as a family. At first, it did, but then it all went downhill because of her. One night her father went to buy her some pampers and formula. We were only fifteen, and he was using his last. He would do anything for Natalia; he loved her so much. Anyway, the store got robbed and he was caught in the crossfire. I'd lost him forever, and I was suddenly a single mother! Ever since then, I treated her like a little sister instead of a daughter, because I'd lost that connection to her," she said and then started to cough.

"Wow, what was his name?" I inquired as I patted her frail back.

"Nate Thomas. We combined our names to come up with Natalia. It was so perfect," she whispered as she stared at the ceiling.

"I'm sorry to hear about him. True love is hard to come by," I shook my head.

"You seem to be in love, you're glowing," Dalia half-smiled.

"Maybe I am," I nodded.

"Who is the lucky guy?" she raised a brow.

"You'll just have to wait and see Ms. Dalia. Now I'm gonna go make you that special tea, and I will be right back," I kissed her forehead and then exited the room.

After making Dalia's tea, I quickly delivered it to her. I told her that I was going to use the bathroom, and then went to find Natalia. I heard her in the laundry room with Winnie, so I waited until I saw Winnie leave with a basket in hand. I quickly slipped into the room and then closed and locked the door behind me.

"Wow Winnie- What are you doing?" Natalia turned to look at me.

"I came for seconds," I smirked and walked closer to her.

"Seconds? River no," she put her hand out to stop me from coming closer, as she backed into the dryer.

"You know you liked it Natalia. Julius will never know, and I'm sure he won't care," I cheesed.

"No River! I said to stop! Get out of here right now!" she yelled and pointed towards the laundry room door.

"Fine Natalia, but it'll only be a matter of time," I exhaled heavily and then rushed out of the room.

I knew she was gonna crack soon, and when she did, my tongue would be ready. I couldn't wait until we became closer. I wanted to taste her all the time and hopefully, she would soon divorce Julius. However, I didn't mind being her dirty little secret for as long as she needed me to.

JULIUS

I'd finally bought a nice ass yacht, and tonight I planned to take my wife on a very romantic date. I knew I'd been working a lot, but it was all for good reason.

It was around 12pm, and I'd just landed in my private jet around thirty minutes ago. I'd stopped and picked up the flowers I ordered for my wife, along with a blueberry diamond ring. I crept into the house and went straight to the bedroom. Natalia wasn't in there, so I stopped by my kids' rooms to check on them.

"Hey beautiful," I whispered as I approached my daughter Harmony's crib.

She was sleeping so peacefully and she was so pretty just like her mother. I was prepared to have to pull my AK out on any little niggas that tried to come within ten feet of her. I kissed her fat cheek and then gently rubbed her back before leaving. I walked into my son Jackson's room, and saw him playing with his toys in his playpen. I chuckled because he was concentrating hard on one of the toys.

"What you doing man?" I knelt down and he looked at me.

He looked just like me, and I knew he would have these hoes eating out the palm of his hand when he got older. I rubbed his head and he giggled. I kissed his cheek and then picked him up to hug him tightly.

"You wanna do something nice for your mommy?" I asked him as he talked his gibberish.

I placed the diamond ring box in his chunky hands, and I held the bouquet of roses in my free hand. We walked downstairs, and I saw Winnie walking towards the kitchen.

"Winnie, where is Nat?" I quizzed.

"Oh Mr. Tate! When did you get here?" she beamed and hugged me.

"Just now," I chuckled.

"Welcome home and Natalia is in the back by the pool," she nodded and then turned on her heels after pinching Jackson's cheek.

"Hold that gift tight buddy," I told Jackson as I adjusted him on my side.

We walked towards the back of the house, and as I got closer, I saw River standing by the glass sliding doors. She seemed to be captivated by something, and I was wondering what it was. I moved a little closer, and I saw Natalia coming out of the pool. She had on a simple white two-piece bathing suit, and her long hair was hanging down her back. Although her stomach was bulging slightly, she still looked extremely sexy.

"Good afternoon River," I said and she jumped. "You like what you see?" I raised a brow.

"Oh no. I was gonna tell her something, but I forgot what it was so I was standing here trying to remember," she lied horribly.

"Right," I laughed and then walked past her outside.

"Julius!" Natalia squealed and ran to me. I handed her the flowers and before I could speak, she got on her tiptoes and pressed her lips against mine. "And what is this cutie?" she said to Jackson as she took the box from his hands. "Julius," she whispered as she admired the blueberry diamond ring. I handed Jackson to her, and pulled the ring out of the box. I slid it onto her finger, and then kissed her full lips.

"You like it?" I asked.

"Yes Ju, of course," she replied in a low tone as her eyes stayed locked on it.

"Good, and tonight we're going on a little date," I winked and she blushed.

"I can't wait. I've missed you," she smiled and leaned her head back for a kiss.

I took Jackson back from her, kissed his cheek, and then grabbed her hand to lead her inside the house. My dick was begging to be inside her right now.

"You cold babe?" I asked Natalia as we drove to the docking area.

"A little," she nodded. I turned the heat on and rubbed her exposed thigh.

We were gonna have a nice romantic date on the new yacht. I wanted to do something nice for her, because I'd been leaving her alone a lot, which I hated to do. Therefore, whenever I came back, I wanted to remind her why she was with me.

"Are we going to the beach? Ju, it's too cold," she whined and rubbed her small bulge.

"We won't be cold, watch," I chuckled as I parked my car.

I got out, and walked around to open the door for her. She threw her shawl around her shoulders so that she could warm up. I grabbed her hand, and we walked down the dock until we reached the large yacht I purchased. She stared at it with her eyes bucked as we walked closer to it. I walked off the dock, and onto the front of the boat while she stood there staring at me.

"Come on ma," I said as I reached my hand out to help her.

"What if I fall in the water?" she giggled.

I shook my head at her, and then climbed back onto the dock. I scooped her up bridal style, and then carried her down onto the boat. I put her down, and then we entered the dining area I had set up on the boat. I pulled her chair out then went around the table to sit down myself.

"This is your boat?" she whispered.

"Well, it's *our* boat," I whispered back. "Why are we whispering?" I raised a brow and she smiled and shrugged.

"Good evening Mr. and Mrs. Tate, my name is Barry, and today I will be the captain on your boat. This will be a smooth ride I promise," he smiled and shook both of our hands before walking away.

"This is our boat?" Natalia quizzed.

"Yeah, when you're married you share everything," I replied as I half-smiled at the chef nearing.

"Mr. and Mrs. Tate, I am Chef Marquis, and I will be cooking your meals this evening. For the appetizer, a Caprese salad will be served. Also, since you are expecting Mrs. Tate we can make any drink virgin," he smiled.

"Okay, can I have a mango margarita?" Natalia cheesed.

"Absolutely, and for you, sir?" he asked.

"I will take a Whiskey Sour," I responded.

"Nice choice. My assistant Meghan will bring those out right away."

"Thank you," Natalia and I said in unison.

"You never cease to amaze me," Natalia smiled.

"Well that's a good thing, because marriage can become very boring I've heard," I exhaled.

"I could never get bored with you," she half-smiled.

"You better not, because I wouldn't let you go."

"Likewise Mr. Tate," she chuckled.

"You're so beautiful baby girl. The baby is giving you a glow too," I said.

"I'm glad you like it. I'm already starting to feel like Shamu," she joked.

"Yeah, I like it. I like everything about you. Someone else seems to as well." I raised a brow and moved back as Meghan set down the salads and drinks.

"What do you mean?" Natalia asked after we prayed over the meal.

"River, she likes you and not just as a friend," I smiled.

"What? W-why would you think that?" she bucked her eyes as she cut the salad.

"Relax ma. And it's because I caught her staring at you when you were swimming earlier," I replied.

"Really?" she turned her lip up.

"Really. You can't blame her though."

"Stop saying that Julius," she pouted.

"Nat, chill out baby I'm joking," I chuckled.

"It's not funny. Let's talk about something else," she spat as she sipped her virgin margarita.

"Umm, alright. How is Harmony's Bake Shoppe coming along?" I inquired.

"It's really great. We're selling at least two hundred cupcakes a day, and bringing in about $1600 a day too," she beamed.

"Damn ma! It's probably because you put crack in them things, and then charge $8 a cupcake," I taunted.

"I'll never tell you my secret ingredient," she grinned.

"I'll just ask you when I'm hitting that spot, you'll tell me anything I wanna hear at that time," I laughed and so did she.

"No I won't!" she smacked her lips.

"Yes the fuck you will. I could ask you to walk to Tokyo, and you'll be whimpering *yess Juuu*," I mocked her and she stared at me with her mouth open.

"I hate you," she shook her head giggling.

"You love me," I sipped my drink.

"I do."

For dinner, we ate sweet tea brined chicken, with loaded mashed potatoes. We had caramelized cannoli for dessert, and Natalia had a decaf vanilla cappuccino.

"I'm so stuffed honey," Natalia sighed and rubbed her stomach.

"I know you are. You vacuumed up all the food before it could even cool," I smiled as I stood up.

"I'm feeding your baby," she replied as she stood up as well.

"I know, thank you," I leaned down and kissed her soft lips.

I took her hand in mine, and led her to the downstairs area of the yacht. Down there was a full master bedroom, with a California king bed. As soon as we walked in, I turned the heat up a little bit since she was shivering. She lifted her hair up and looked over her shoulder to tell me to unzip her dress. I walked up behind her and slid the zipper down slowly. The dress glided down her small frame and hit the floor. She stepped out of it, and turned to face me with her small, round, perky titties sitting up nicely. I admired her beauty from head to toe, as I unbuttoned my shirt. She unbuckled my pants, and let them drop so I could step out of them. I leaned down to kiss her, and then went from her neck to her breasts, and then her stomach. While on my knees, I tugged down her black lace thong, and kissed her growing stomach again. I sat her down on the bed, and spread her legs slowly so that I could take in the beauty of her center. I rested her smooth peanut butter thighs on my shoulders, and inhaled the sweet scent of her pussy.

"Mmmm," she tucked her lips in as she moaned.

I pecked her lower lips gently and repeatedly. I then swiped my tongue between the slit very slowly, causing another moan to escape her mouth. She was getting wetter and wetter as I continued to switch back and forth between pecking and swiping. I was starting to see a glisten when I parted the lips, so I knew she was ready. I took her clit into my mouth, and sucked it very gently, making her arch her back. I caressed her thighs while I feasted on her vagina. Her juices were spilling out by the second, and I was slurping it all up.

"Juuu, shit," she shivered as she came.

I kept going, because as usual, I could never get enough. I plunged my finger into her hole, while sucking her harder. She spread her legs further apart, and reached down to caress the back of my head just the way I liked her to.

"Juu, you're so good at this," she whimpered as I pushed her legs back for more access. "Oh, oh my gooshhh," she cried out while trying to catch her breath.

I kept sucking, licking, and slurping until she let loose again. I licked her clean, and stood up to take my boxer briefs off. As soon as I did, my dick sprang up, staring her right in the face. She made eye contact with me, and then took me into her warm wet mouth. She made love to the tip, letting her mouth become full of spit. She took the rest of my dick into her mouth and began to massage my balls as she bobbed. She was doing a sloppy job, and it was taking me over the edge.

"Shit," I mumbled as I looked down at her. She was so into it, and that shit was sexy as hell.

I busted my nut, and she swallowed it like a professional. I laid on my back, and she mounted my rod. She slid down on it slowly, and winced in pain. Once she was all the way down, a moan burst through both our lips. I ran my hands from her plump ass cheeks, up her back, and around to her breasts. I pinched her nipples, and bit my lip as I watched her sex faces appear.

"Ahh, ahhh," she purred while placing her small hand on my abs.

"Keep doing that shit just like that Nat," I cheered her on before smacking and grabbing her ass.

She rocked her hips and bounced on me slowly, making us both cry out in pleasure. I wondered if the chef and waitress could hear us, but I didn't care if they could.

"Urrgghhh," Natalia grunted softly as she came, and then collapsed on me.

I pulled her bottom lip into my mouth and then we started to suck one another's lips. I flipped her over on her back, leaving my dick inside her. She locked her arms around my neck as we continued to let our tongues dance together. She wrapped her legs around my waist as well, as I thrust into her in a circular motion.

"Uhhh, uhhh," she cooed into my mouth. "I love you so much Julius," she whispered as we kissed passionately.

She caressed the back of my head and I hugged her body a little tighter. We were so close to each other that we were almost one. I loved this woman so much it was crazy. The little girl that I ran into at CVS had become the love of my life; that shit crept up on my ass like a muthafucka. It's funny because, that day I didn't wanna even stop there, but Greg and Bianca damn near begged me to.

"Ahh, ahhh, ooooh," she moaned in a high-pitched voice.

"Mmmm," I groaned as I shot my seeds up into her body.

We laid there sweating because of the sex and the heater I'd turned on when we first walked in.

"Thank you," she whispered.

"For what?" I questioned.

"For loving me when no one else did," she replied as she caressed my face and stared up into my eyes.

"And thank you for loving me when I didn't deserve to be loved."

I dipped my tongue back into her mouth, as we embraced one another. I guess God had brought us together because we unknowingly needed each other.

NATALIA

"Harmony's Bake Shoppe, this is Natalia," I sang into the phone.

"Yes, I'd like to place an order for seventy cupcakes. Thirty-five blueberry cheesecake and the other half, almond with the earl grey butter cream," the guy replied.

"Braxton?" I smiled.

"How could you tell?" he quizzed.

"Well, you didn't try to disguise your voice," I chuckled.

"I know, I know. But I really wanna place that order," he replied.

"When do you need it?" I asked.

"In two weeks, for my baby mother's birthday."

"Oh, well that's nice of you," I nodded as I wrote down the details.

"Yeah, we aren't together or anything," he said.

"Why did you say it like that? I don't care," I frowned. We were just associates, yet he was telling me this as if we were building something.

"Oh yes, I forgot you're off limits," he sighed.

"Very. Now are there any specific little decorations you'd like on the cupcakes? Or just top them with frosting?" I inquired.

"If you guys could put something on it that would be great," he responded.

"Alright, is this delivery or pick up?"

"Would you be delivering them if I chose delivery?" he questioned in a flirty tone.

"Braxton," I said in a serious tone. All this flirting from him and River was annoying the fuck out of me. Don't people have any respect for marriage anymore?

"I'm sorry, I'm sorry I had to," he chuckled. "But I can pick them up."

"Okay, so the cupcakes are $560, plus $50 for the decorations placed on each. So you're looking at $610," I told him.

"That's perfectly fine."

"Okay, and we take a fifty percent deposit before we start. So I would have to collect $305 before we begin baking, I folded my arms and waited for his response.

"Look at you Ms. Business woman. I have a card here," he giggled and I rolled my eyes.

After taking his card number over the phone and tying up the details, I was ready to go home. I had to work on some other recipes and I wanted to be done by the time Julius called me. I hated that he was in Indiana all the time, but I knew he had to work. He only stayed there three days out of the week, but it seemed like way more.

"Natalia, this just came," my employee Nikki walked in with a huge bouquet of roses.

"Oh my gosh, who are they from?" I asked.

"Not sure," she shrugged and then skated off to the front.

Just a little something to say I love you and miss you. Julius, the note read.

I squealed and then sniffed the flowers. Despite our extremely rocky start together, he was the greatest in the world.

"Okay ladies, we have another bulk order, but it's not due for two weeks, so we will start at 5am on the day it is supposed to be done," I told the girls and my new baking/managing assistant Latoya.

"Got it. Have a good day Natalia," they all replied in unison.

After feeding, bathing, and spending time with my babies, it was time to work. It was already 5pm, and I knew I needed to start testing the new flavors I wanted to put into the store. If they came out perfect tonight, then I could possibly have them in by the end of the week.

"Hello Natalia, I haven't seen you all day," River entered the kitchen.

"Oh yeah, I went to the bakery around 5:30am this morning," I replied not taking my eyes off the ingredients.

"Hard worker," she nodded. "What are you doing now?" she quizzed.

"I'm baking these new flavors I came up with," I responded making sure not to make eye contact.

"Oh, can I taste?" she questioned as I pulled the first two trays out of the oven.

"Umm, sure," I said as I put them in the freezer to cool. Couldn't she just go away?

"When is Julius coming back?" she asked.

"In two days."

"I see. Do you get lonely at night?" she smirked.

"River-"

"It's a valid question. We're friends. I'm sure Lucy asks things like that," she cut in.

"I, uh, yeah sometimes I do but it's very rare," I fake smiled and then pulled the cupcakes down. I frosted the two different flavors and put them on a little plate. "This one is the pineapple habanero cupcake, with a pineapple coconut frosting. The other one is a honey jalapeno cornbread cupcake, with a fresh cream frosting," I told River as I slid her a little plate containing two.

"This is so good!" she beamed while covering her mouth since she had a mouth full.

"It is," I chuckled after tasting for myself.

"Yes! You're so good at this cupcake thing," she grinned.

"Well thank you," I laughed.

She stood up after finishing and then walked closer to me. She walked past me, set the plate in the sink and then came up and grabbed me from behind.

"River move," I said in a low tone.

"Natalia, just one more time," she whispered as she rubbed up my thigh, and tugged gently on my panties.

"No," I panted as I felt her swipe her fingers across my wet vagina.

She pulled my panties down roughly, dropped down and then began to lick my pussy from the back. What the fuck was I doing? She lifted and separated my butt cheeks, then sucked harder on my clit. I grabbed onto the counter and threw my head back in ecstasy. I prayed that Winnie was in her room and not wandering around.

"Mmmm," I tucked my lips in to muffle my moans, as she continued to feast on me.

She spread my thighs wider, and sucked harder while moaning herself. It felt way too good to stop now. She darted her tongue into my hole, making me grunt softly.

"Shit," I mumbled.

"Cum in my mouth Nat," she said in between slurps and sucks.

"Uhhhh," I cooed in a soft voice as I released. She licked me clean as if her tongue was a wet wipe, and then flicked her tongue over my clit.

"So tasty, mmm," she commented as she started to slowly suck my clit again.

By this time, I was completely bent over the counter biting my lip. Every now and then, I tried to keep my eyes open to make sure no one walked in. She made love to my clit, and licked around the hole every now and then. She wasn't as good as Julius, but this would do for now.

"Ahhh, ahhh, oh my gosh," I squealed before finally cumming again.

She licked it all up, and then slowly stood to her feet. She leaned down on me and kissed my neck, while rubbing her fingers over my sopping wet pussy.

"It could always be like this when he's away. I would never tell," she whispered into my ear, while plunging her fingers into me from behind until I came again.

At first, it sounded good, but then I came to my senses. Julius and I were doing so well, and I *would* be the person to fuck it up. He had to forgive me though, because I forgave him countless times. I forgave him for hitting me, and cheating on me numerous times, so this shouldn't be a problem. She wasn't even a guy!

"No River. Go home," I nudged her off me, and then picked my thong up from the floor.

"But Natalia-"

"Go home River, damn!" I shouted and pushed her out of the kitchen, all the way to the door.

"I need my purse!" she yelled as I slammed the door.

I ran to my mother's room, and tried to slip on my panties on the way. River pounded on the door as I entered my mom's room and grabbed her purse. I ran back to the door and threw it in her face before slamming the door closed again.

"Natalia, baby, are you alright?" Winnie asked as she looked over the stair balcony.

"Yes, yeah, I'm fine," I smiled and rushed back to the kitchen to clean up.

I hurriedly cleaned the area while eating one of the cupcakes, and then went to my room to take a bath. I needed to get my shit together. This was not me. I was not a cheater! Julius couldn't find out and if he did, he couldn't leave me. I loved him and I was carrying his third baby, he couldn't just *not* love me anymore.

JULIUS

All this traveling back and forth was really fucking with me. I was starting to hate planes altogether. I just had to suck it up though, because as they say, *you have to pay the cost to be the boss*.

I was home now though and couldn't wait to lay up with my girl. I usually told her when I was coming, but I enjoyed the look on her face when I surprised her every now and then. I walked through the foyer with some sunflowers. Sunflowers meant adoration, loyalty, and longevity and that was everything I wanted my marriage to be full of.

As I was approaching the stairs, I heard soft moans coming from the laundry room area. I was confused because I highly doubted that Winnie or Dalia would be fucking in my crib. For one, Winnie was up there in age, and Dalia was too damn sick to even walk on her own, let alone be fucking. I got closer to the door, and the moans sounded all too familiar. A part of me was scared to push open the door, because I didn't know if I could fathom what I was about to see. *Man up Julius*, I told myself.

I took a deep breath, and pushed the door open slowly. Natalia was standing against the dryer, and River was on her knees eating her pussy. Natalia's eyes were closed, and her head was thrown back so she had no idea I was watching.

The sight before me didn't turn me on like it would have done most niggas. I was disgusted. Here I was busting my ass working and making sure that I stayed faithful to my wife, even though I knew she would never know if I cheated, and she was back home fucking on her mother's nurse. She was pregnant with my child, and getting ate out by some random bitch like a local hood rat.

"Sorry to interrupt," I said and they both jumped.

"Julius!" Natalia called out, and grabbed her underwear from off the top of the washing machine next to her. River wiped her mouth, and just darted her eyes from me to Natalia repeatedly.

"Nah, continue," I smirked and then turned to walk away.

"Julius!" Natalia yelled as she followed me. I didn't say anything as I climbed the stairs. "Julius, I'm sorry I-" I shoved the flowers into her chest, cutting her sentence off.

Once we reached the top of the stairs, I went into the room to pack my shit. I wasn't sure if I was gonna stay in the guest room or go to the condo I had, but I wouldn't be staying here with this hoe.

"Baby, talk to me! I'm sorry! It's not what you think!" she started to cry.

"Let's see, while I'm working, you're back here fucking someone else. That's pretty clear to me Nat," I chuckled.

"Where are you going?" she asked, as her face became covered in tears.

"I'm leaving you," I scoffed.

"No Julius, stop! Please! It's not like that! She kept coming after me!" she sobbed hysterically.

"And you think bitches ain't been coming after me? Don't come at me with that bullshit ass excuse Natalia! You wanna fuck on her then you can be with her ass! I'm done with you! It's a fucking wrap and ain't shit you can say to change my mind!" I shouted.

"Julius no, we have a baby on the way," she got in front of me to block me from leaving with my bag.

"I'm gonna take care of my kid, but I'm not gone be with yo' ass. You ain't nothing but a little sneaky ass hoe, like I've always suspected. You're fucking pregnant and you over here letting her eat you out.

Just like a fucking whore. I should've never left Bianca for you," I said hoping to hurt her like she'd done me.

"What? How could you say that? I thought you loved me?" she sniffled.

"I thought you loved me too, but now I'm seeing that ain't the fucking case. Now get the fuck out of my way!" I hollered.

"No! So you can go cheat? I'm not letting you! I said I was sorry Julius! I've forgiven you so many times," she wailed like a newborn baby.

"I don't give a fuck! What, you forgave me so that you could have a pass in the future?" I turned my lip up.

"No, I forgave you because I loved you and I wanted to be with you. The same thing you should do right now," she cried.

"Well, I'm not," I replied and slipped past her.

She chased after me as I booked it down the stairs. She was grabbing my shirt and my arm, but she wasn't strong enough to stop me from moving. I didn't know if I was just that strong or if the anger inside me made me that way.

"Julius!" she sobbed like she was dying. "Please baby I'm sorry!" she begged through tears. She had some nerve crying this hard because she thought I was about to cheat, when she was just getting licked on by someone else.

"Let me go Natalia!" I shouted as I tried to pry her small hands from my shirt.

"No Julius, please I-"

"Ain't nobody about to cheat on you, now let me go dammit!" I hit the wall and shouted so loud that it rumbled in my chest.

She didn't say anything; she just looked at me and then at the big ass hole in the wall. She let my shirt loosen from her hands and I stormed out.

"When are you coming back?" she yelled after me.

I didn't say anything and slid into my car. I sped to the condo, as Natalia blew my phone up the whole way. By the time I got there, I had forty missed calls and fifteen text messages from her only. I blocked her number, and then put my phone on silent so no one else could contact me. When I got inside, I pulled a big bottle of Hennessy from the bar and grabbed a cup.

I was overwhelmed with so many emotions. How could she do this shit to me? After all that we'd been through, and after all the promises we made to each other, she betrayed me. There were so many hoes from here to Indiana throwing their pussy my way, and I turned it all down for her hoe ass.

Suddenly the condo phone rang, but I saw it was her on the caller I.D, so I didn't pick up. I turned the TV on, and decided to just relax and watch TV, to give me some time to think. At this point, I loved Natalia, but I didn't want to be with her. It wasn't the cheating that was bothering me as much, it was the sneakiness behind it. I didn't feel like I could trust her at all anymore. All the times I accused her of cheating, she probably was. I shook my head and downed my drink before refilling it. My phone lit up next to me, and I relaxed when I saw it was my brother Rashad.

"Hello," I answered and took a sip of my drink.

"Luke and Jabari said only a quarter shipment came in this morning," Rashad said somberly.

"What the fuck you mean only a quarter?" I frowned and slammed my glass down.

"Just what I said. We only got twenty-five percent of what we usually get," he huffed. "I don't know what happened man. I thought you would've had a reason for it," he added.

"What? Hell nah! Why would I only have a portion come in?" I turned my lip up as if he could see me.

"He said the guy told him that was all that was requested."

"Aight, I'll hit you back in a few," I replied before disconnecting.

I knew this was Skylar's doing. I should've known that since she wasn't bothering me, she was up to some bullshit. Like I said before, I was tired of making threats, today I was making good on them.

I polished off my last sips of Hennessy, and then jogged to my car. I sped straight to Bart's home, and barely parked the car before getting out. This bitch had me fucked up, and it was the wrong day for her to piss me off. I knew she did this, because Bart was still in

Peru. His mother lived longer than expected, so he extended his stay.

BOOM!

BOOM!

BOOM!

I banged on the door repeatedly, until I heard someone opening the locks. I was prepared to go the fuck off, but Bart's other daughter, Leah walked out.

"Oh, hi Julius. I was just leaving, but say hi to Natalia for me," she smiled and started to walk off.

"Fasho, is your sister inside?" I asked.

"Yes, she's in the theatre," she replied and hopped into her Mercedes.

"Thanks," I said even though I knew she couldn't hear me.

I closed and locked the front door after putting my gloves on, and then walked to the theatre room to look for Skylar. As soon as I walked in, I saw her chilling with some little ass shorts on. Her ass was hanging out the bottom and my dick took notice. I should've been fucked her, since Natalia wanted to be a hoe.

"Julius, hey boo," she winked.

"What happened to the shipment bitch?" I spat.

"I would appreciate it if you didn't call me a bitch Ju," she giggled like the weirdo she was.

"Look bitch, I need to know where the fuck the rest of my shipment is. If you don't speak the fuck up, I'm deadin' you right here and right now," I stated sternly.

"Well, since you couldn't return my calls, I felt that maybe you didn't need as much product," she smacked her lips and put her hand on her hip.

"One has nothing to do with the other."

"It does when I'm in charge. I told you before Julius, if you want this business relationship to work, all you have to do is share the wealth," she cheesed and rubbed her hand against my dick.

"Oh, that's all you wanted?" I bit my lip and she nodded.

"Pretty please, with a cherry on top."

Usually I would've let her dome me up, but I wasn't in the mood. Natalia had fucked my whole day up and I just wanted to be alone more than anything right now. So, that meant I needed to get this over with.

"Well, make whatever calls you need to make in order to get the rest of the product here by tomorrow night and we got a deal," I said.

"Oh no honey, I need the dick first," she cocked her head.

"You'll get it after. Now make the fucking call," I replied as I tapped her face with my gun.

"You better be glad I like it rough," she sighed and then pulled her phone out.

"On speaker," I demanded and she did so. I listened as she set everything up.

"Okay, it's all-"

PHEW!

PHEW!

I quickly pumped two in her dome, and she collapsed to the ground. Leese and Dash finally arrived and quickly cleaned her out for disposal. I knew I would have to take Bart out next. Today was just not my fucking day.

NATALIA

Depressed was an understatement. If I wasn't working or spending time with my kids and mom, I was in the bed crying. It'd only been three days, but it felt like an eternity. Someone that I was used to talking to or seeing all the time, I hadn't seen or talked to at all. There were no texts or calls of any kind. I called from every number possible because I knew mine was blocked, and I still got no answer.

"Natalia are you-" River peeped her head into my bedroom.

"Get out!" I shouted to her and pointed to the door.

Ever since Julius caught us, I'd been keeping her ass away. I was so mad at myself for letting her do what she did three damn times. At least if she was someone I was interested in I would feel better, but she wasn't. I cheated on my husband with someone I didn't give two fucks about. Yeah I used her for a quick orgasm, but so what, she let me.

"River, I said- Oh Winnie, what's up?" I sat up when I heard the door creak again.

"Baby, Julius is here to see the kids. I wasn't sure if you wanted to know," she half-smiled.

"Yes, thank you. Where is he?" I asked.

"He's in the den playing with them," she replied and then walked out.

I ran to the bathroom and washed my face to remove the tearstains. I slipped into some tights, because my jeans weren't quite fitting my waist anymore. I was five months, but I wasn't showing that much unless I was naked. I put a t-shirt on and then put my hair into a ponytail. I rushed down the stairs and to the den. I stopped in my tracks when I saw his beautiful caramel face. His facial hair was trimmed perfectly and his hair was freshly cut. He was wearing gray sweats and a white t-shirt with a black Jordan jump man on it. His shoes were off, showing his black socks. He watched Jackson play with his blocks, while holding Harmony in his lap.

"Hi," I said in a low tone.

"What's up," he replied without looking at me.

"Where have you been?" I questioned.

"Why?" he frowned.

"Because, I missed you. I wanted to know where you've been," I half-smiled.

"Well, you don't need to worry about that. I'm leaving to Indiana tonight anyway," he spat.

"Then can we talk?"

"I'm spending time with my kids right now, so no," he responded.

"I mean in like an hour or two. I can make you some spicy barbecue wings for lunch," I cheesed.

"I'll pass," he sighed.

"When are we gonna talk Julius?" I whined.

"There ain't shit to talk about. You cheated and now I don't want you," he scoffed. His words cut like a freshly sharpened knife.

"You don't want me? So you're not in love with me anymore?" I inquired on the verge of crying.

"Not really. I care about you but I don't love you," he looked up at me and nodded. A couple tears ran down my cheeks, but I wiped them quickly.

"Oh," was all I managed to get out before I left the room.

I couldn't make it to my room, so I slipped into the bathroom and burst into tears. Why couldn't he forgive me? After just three days, he was out of love? How is that even possible? I grabbed some tissues and cried into them as my body jerked lightly. This was one of the worst things that could ever happen to me. I came out of the bathroom and went upstairs to lie down for a nap. I didn't bother to change into my nightgown, I just took my ponytail down and passed out.

I woke up, and the room was a little darker than it was when I initially fell asleep. I picked up my phone and replied to some messages from Lucy, and Victoria from back in Indiana. Suddenly the door opened, and Julius came in. I sat up, and put my phone on the nightstand.

"How is the baby?" he asked as he leaned up against the door.

"It's fine, the doctor just said I need to stop stressing," I replied in a low tone.

"Then maybe you should do that," he exhaled as he walked to the chair and sat down.

"I can't right now," I said.

"You should at least try," he shook his head.

"I do try, but I can't help that I'm sad," I whispered.

"Maybe your little nurse cuddy buddy can make you feel better," he shrugged and looked at his phone.

"I don't want her Julius. She just caught me in a vulnerable moment! I was lonely here, and she was there; always complimenting me, and pressing up on me," I cried.

"That's all it takes to get a piece, huh? A few nice words and persistence. Nice," he chuckled and shook his head. "Sounds just like a little easy hoe," he smirked.

"Yeah, keep calling your children's mother a hoe," I sniffled.

"Niggas have hoes for baby mamas all the time," he taunted with his beautiful smile plastered on his face.

"I guess you've joined the club then," I exhaled.

"I guess I have," he nodded as if he was sure of his statement.

"So, are we getting a divorce or what?" I quizzed.

"Most likely. Why, are you ready to make it official with River?" he chuckled.

I just turned my back to him and let the tears fall where they may. I wasn't gonna wipe them either. My body slightly jerked, but no sound came out as I stared at his side of the bed.

"Take care of my baby," he patted my back and headed for the door.

"I hate you!" I shouted. "You treated me like shit for the longest and I forgave you every single time! You forced me to get an abortion, cheated on me with any girl that looked your way, and hit me for no reason at all, and every time I took you back with no questions asked! Yet this one little time that I messed up, you act like it's the end of the world! You left me here three days a week by myself, so yes I got lonely and made a dumb ass mistake, but Julius it will never happen again! I was stupid and I'm sorry but you can't just leave me!" I yelled.

"How do I know that you won't get lonely again, but this time let a nigga fuck? Huh? How the fuck do I know that?" he frowned and pointed his finger in his chest.

"You have to trust that I love you, just like I trusted you every time you lied and said it wouldn't happen again. I trusted you even though time after time it was the same damn story. I believed that one day you would realize what you had and become a good man and thank God, I was right! So Ju, you need to trust that I'm telling the truth. As long as I live, I will never be with anyone else but you, no matter what. I will always love you and be loyal to you no matter what happens," I sobbed. "No matter how many times you've broken my heart; I always forgave you because I loved you. If you're out of love with me already Julius, I need you to try to fall again," I added as tears ran down my already wet face.

He didn't say anything; he just sat down in the room chair again. He ran his hands over his face, and closed his eyes. I slid my tights off, and then climbed out of the bed. It was kind of dark in the room, but I could see just fine because of the window.

I pushed him back so he could sit up, and then straddled his lap. I lifted his shirt off to expose his chiseled body. I removed my big t-shirt, and then kissed softly on his chest while caressing the back of his head. He put his big hands on my belly, as I kissed on his neck. He cupped my breasts, and then began to suck my nipples gently. I continued to caress his head as I threw my head back in pleasure. While keeping his mouth latched onto my nipple, he tugged my panties down. I hadn't felt him in forever, and the anticipation alone had me dripping. To keep me from having to get out of his lap, he ripped my underwear from my thighs. I pulled his sweats and boxers down just enough to expose his dick, and then positioned myself above it. I tongued him down slowly and nastily, as I slid down on him. I was going inch by inch because his massiveness was a lot to handle after so long. I hugged him tightly, and moaned into his mouth when I finally had him all the way inside me.

"I'm sorry baby, I love you," he whispered into my mouth as I slowly bounced on his dick.

He put my legs over his forearms without breaking our kiss, so that he could have more access to my opening. The last few times we'd had sex had been so much more than physical and I loved it. Our bodies were making love spiritually and physically, which made the orgasm much greater.

"Fuck you're so tight and wet," he said in a low tone.

"Only for you," I said in between our passionate kisses. "I love you Ju, I'll never do anything again," I added as we sucked each other's lips.

He may have broken his promises to me in the past, but I was gonna make good on mine.

I had some serious making up to do. I should've never made her sweat like that, having to call me forty and fifty times. I knew Natalia loved me more than anything, but I was just disappointed in her. She'd always been down for me and it just hurt to see her betray me. But at the end of the day, I loved her and she didn't need to be stressing while carrying my baby.

"Good morning baby girl," I walked into the bedroom carrying a tray of pancakes, eggs, fruit, turkey sausage, and juice.

"Julius, I thought you were supposed to go to Indiana," she half-smiled as she wiped the sleep from her eyes. She pulled the sheet up to cover her naked body, as I sat the tray across her lap.

"I know and I was, but I decided to stay some extra days," I smiled.

"I'm not gonna do anything, so you can go if you need to," she said biting the sausage.

"I know you're not ma, I just wanted to spend some extra time with you," I moved her hair out of her face as she scarfed down the pancakes. "Damn you must be starved," I commented sarcastically.

"Yeah," she chuckled nervously.

"After I have my phone meeting, me, you, and the babies can go to

Fiery Ron's. I know you like that place when you're pregnant," I offered.

"I can't wait," she blushed. "I love you Julius," she whispered as she looked into my eyes.

"I love you too Natalia," I tongued her down while palming her small belly.

"Ju, I haven't brushed my teeth," she pulled back and covered her mouth.

"It's not even bad, come here," I chuckled and moved the empty tray out of the way.

"Nooo," she giggled.

"I love everything about you, even your breath in the morning," I said before dipping my tongue back into her mouth again.

"You're so nasty," she snickered in between kisses.

I needed to speak with Antonio, my other connect, about possibly fulfilling Bart's shipment from now on. I knew I had one more shipment coming from Bart, but after that, it would be a wrap. I knew he would find out about his daughter, and immediately suspect me. I was ready though, and unfortunately, I would have to end his life too.

I walked into my office, closed the door and dialed Antonio.

"Julius Tate, my favorite distributor," Antonio sang into the phone.

"What's up man, I need to talk to you," I sighed.

"I hope it's nothing bad," he said.

"It depends on how you take it. Look, my original connect is no more and I need you to provide product for South Carolina too," I told him.

"That's it? Man, I been told you I could supply you for both areas. You were just trying to be loyal to that cat," Antonio chuckled.

"Well, all that shit is over," I responded.

"And that is definitely good news for me."

"Cool. Now, I need three times what I get now. I prefer as little pick up days as possible," I said.

"Alright, let me just set some things up and then I will call you back with the details my friend," he coughed.

"Sounds good," I replied and then disconnected.

As if he had extreme intuitive powers, my phone rang and Bart's name flashed across. I took a deep breath and then finally answered the call.

"Hello?"

"Where is my daughter Julius?" he asked and I could tell his teeth were clenched.

"Which one?" I taunted.

"Skylar! Leah said she hasn't been home in days!" he shouted.

"I see... well sorry Bart I have no idea where she is. If anything comes up, I will definitely give you a call," I said.

"Well until she comes up, you won't have any shipments coming in after the one tomorrow," he spat.

"That's unfortunate Bart," I shrugged.

"Yes, especially since I'll be distributing to Brax. I'm sure he will be reigning in no time with me behind him," he laughed and my blood started to boil.

"Great business move Bart. Have a good one," I told him before quickly hanging up.

I wasn't worried about Brax at all. I planned to kill his ass too, so there wasn't shit to worry about. I was just waiting for him to strike again. He had better hope he didn't try anything with my wife or I would make his ass suffer for sure.

BRAXTON NORTHLAND

I woke up and heard rustling behind me. I knew it was Sonia's ass getting dressed for something. I looked over my shoulder and spotted her getting her things together for the shower. I didn't know what her ass was up to, but I knew she was on some sneaky shit. For the past few weeks, she was always looking at that fucking phone and giggling like a fucking schoolgirl.

"Where are you going birthday girl?" I smiled as I wiped my eyes.

"Well, I was thinking we could hang out now because I have plans later on tonight," she replied.

"With whom? I thought I could take you to dinner tonight," I frowned. Tonight was the surprise party for her, which is why I purchased the cupcakes.

"I know babe, but I kind of want to hang out with my girls tonight," she said.

"For what? When I was in jail for seven years, you hung with them on all those birthdays! This is your first birthday that I've been able to spend with you in a while Sonia!" I shouted.

"Take your voice down first of all nigga. Secondly, that's why I'm letting you take me to lunch," she beamed and then floated off to the bathroom.

I hopped out of the bed and then went to take a shower in the other bathroom. Regardless if there was a party or not, I wanted to pick up those cupcakes. Not only did I pay a fifty percent deposit for them already, but I kind of wanted to see Natalia also. I knew it would never be anything, and I'm sure Julius wouldn't go down without a fight over her but it was nothing wrong with looking.

As I walked into the bedroom with my towel wrapped around my waist, I heard the door slam, and saw my wallet open on the bed. I shook my head because I knew Sonia had just left to go shopping with my damn bankcard. I got dressed, brushed my teeth and then went into the safe to get some cash for the cupcakes. I slid into my Porsche, and had to pause for a minute because my head was hurting. I'd just gotten my cornrows freshly braided just for this day, and that bitch didn't even have the decency to spend it with me. I exhaled heavily, and then sped out of the driveway.

"Welcome to Harmony's Bake Shoppe!" one of the pretty, little workers cheesed.

I licked my lips because she was definitely on my list of knock-downs. Yeah, I was in a relationship, but what man stuck with one woman? She blushed and looked away once I winked at her.

"I'm here to pick up an order for Braxton Northland," I said to her. Natalia emerged from the back looking scrumptious as fuck.

"Oh good morning Braxton," she smirked and folded her arms. She had on a tight nude dress, and for the first time, I saw she was pregnant.

"Good morning Ms. Natalia. You look beautiful today," I bit my lip.

"Thank you. Casey should be bringing your cupcakes out any minute now," she smiled.

A young lady came from the back carrying two big boxes and set them down on the counter. The fine one that I planned to bang out let me know there was a remaining balance of $305.00. I paid that while keeping my eyes on Natalia.

"Can I get a friendly hug before I go?" I asked.

"Umm, sure," Natalia responded and came from behind the

counter. I wrapped my arms around her small body and had to talk myself out of grabbing her little plump ass.

"Fuck off my wife homie," Julius said calmly as he appeared from behind me. Natalia jumped back out of my arms and stared up at him.

"Julius I wasn't-"

"Come to the back," he told her and stormed to the back of the bakery.

"Bye beautiful!" I called after her but she just followed him.

I wasn't tripping off Julius, because I'd just hooked up with his old connect, and I knew we would be taking over soon. Shit, he was the king of Indianapolis and Charleston, why did he need Orangeburg too? Whatever his reasons were, he was gonna give me back my area and bow out gracefully.

"The mall was packed!" Sonia panted as she walked through the door with a bunch of bags.

"Yeah, it was packed daddy!" my daughter Tracie ran to me and hugged me. Tracie was my world, but I knew she would grow up to be just like her mother. Although a very smart woman, Sonia was a rat at heart.

"Oh really, so where are you and your friends going tonight?" I asked Sonia.

"Oh just to the club," she shrugged one shoulder and then plopped on the couch to go through her bags.

"Maybe Billy and I could come with y'all and make it a little group thing," I offered.

"No, it's a girls' night boo. But I promise I'm gonna come home to you and make your toes curl," she winked.

"Yeah, a'ight," I shook my head and sipped my beer. "Take these damn cupcakes with you. Them muthafuckas cost me over a half of a grand," I spat and she and Tracie ran over to the table to inspect them.

"This cheesecake one is bomb babe," Sonia wallowed.

"I like it too daddy," Tracie rushed back over to me holding the cupcake and with frosting on her face.

I pulled my phone out, and went into my email. I clicked Natalia's email and sent her a little something. She needed a boss like me anyway, not a little boy like Julius.

Me: Hey, is everything alright? Didn't mean to cause any problems.

I sent it and leaned my head back with a smile.

"If you're gonna take me to lunch let's go. I need enough time to get ready for tonight," Sonia spat snapping me out of my fantasy with Natalia.

"Come on," I smacked my lips, and then picked up my daughter.

THIRTY MINUTES EARLIER

"Nat, I told you to cease all forms of contact with that nigga!" Julius shouted.

"Julius I know, but he just wanted to buy cupcakes. That was it!" I whined as I watched him sit down. "It was just a hug," I added as I rubbed his soft fade.

"I know," he sighed and pulled me down into his lap. "But make that the last time. No more orders or anything."

"It'll be the last time. Can I ask why?" I questioned while rubbing the nape of his neck.

"He ain't who you think he is and he's only getting at you to fuck with me," he replied and I nodded. I wanted to know more details but I knew he would get angry with me.

I leaned down to kiss his full lips and during our passionate encounter, my computer chimed. We both looked at it and then I got up to click my email client. I saw it was an email from Braxton, so I quickly closed it.

"Another order?" Julius inquired.

"Yep," I lied and smiled.

After being at the shop for a couple more hours, Julius dropped me off at home. He said he had some business to handle and that he would be home very late. It seemed like if he wasn't in Indianapolis, he was doing something all day that didn't involve me.

I walked into the house, and I saw River handing some bed sheets to Winnie for her to wash. My mother was getting worse and it seemed like every day she was ruining a new pair of sheets.

"Hello Natalia," she smirked after Winnie walked off.

"Hi River, it's 4:50pm, shouldn't you be getting ready to leave?" I questioned.

"Yes, but I had to take the sheets off your mother's bed," she fidgeted.

"Oh well, have a good evening," I said as I walked up the stairs to go check on my babies.

I played with Jackson for a little while, and then gave him a bath and some warm milk. He fell right asleep. Winnie had already put Harmony to bed, so I didn't have to worry about her. I wanted them to be sleep because I was about to take a nap. I wanted to be wide-awake when Julius came home, and have enough energy to tend to them when they awakened in the middle of the night.

As I was undressing, I heard my bedroom door open. I looked over my shoulder, and saw River coming in with a big smile on her face. Boy was she persistent, and very annoying.

"You were supposed to be gone an hour ago," I said as I brushed my hair down.

"I know, but I wanted to spend a little time with you before I left," she said and sat down in the room chair.

"For what River? What do you think is going on here?" I questioned and sat my brush down.

"You and I are having an affair," she grinned.

"We are not having an affair River. I've never even kissed you, how would that come off to you as an affair?" I cocked my head.

"We made love though," she chuckled nervously.

"No, you ate my pussy. That was it," I shrugged.

"But the things you said to me. You said I was pretty, a-and that the person I was meant to be with was waiting on me! You said my ex

Cameron wasn't good enough! I knew you were talking about your-self when you said the right person was waiting!" she started to cry.

"River no, I meant someone *else* was the right person. I'm married and most importantly, I'm not a lesbian," I frowned in confusion.

"Me either, but that can change. You changed me Natalia," she pleaded.

"I'm flattered but I haven't changed. I am very much in love with my husband, and if you'd like to continue to work for my husband and I, you're gonna have to stop with all this," I said.

"Why did you let me do what I did?" she squinted her eyes.

"I was horny and I missed my husband. I'm sorry for using you River, I shouldn't have done that," I replied.

"You can't just use people Natalia," she said through gritted teeth.

"I know River. I'm sorry but what do you want me to do?" I frowned.

"You have to be with me! I'm not someone you can use!" she screamed.

"River you need to calm down. I said I was sorry and I don't know what else to tell you. I'm not gonna be with you," I stood up.

"You used me knowing I'd just been broken up with! You're a horrible person Natalia!" she sobbed. I felt so bad after hearing her say that.

"What can I do River? Maybe I can talk to your ex, or set you up," I half-smiled.

"I already told you the only way to fix it is for us to be together and we're gonna be," she grimaced and then stormed out.

SONIA COLEMAN

THAT NIGHT

I was putting the finishing touches on my makeup for my little birthday celebration tonight. I was so anxious to go to this little kickback that Julius was throwing for me. Recently he and I had become real close and tonight we would finally be fucking. I'd been damn near begging for the dick, but he told me that he really liked me and didn't wanna rush. Ain't that something? I loved a nigga who treated everybody else like shit, but treated me like gold. I knew Julius was married to some little hoe he met back in Indiana, but I really did not care. All the texts that he sent to my phone showed he didn't care about her ass either.

I put my Kim Kardashian lip kit away, just as my phone started to ring. I looked down and saw it was my home girl, Shatan. She and my other best friend Lindy were coming through with me since Julius had his homeboys there. It was gonna be very intimate and sexy, and I couldn't wait.

"So you gone?" my boyfriend Brax asked me as my daughter Tracie slept in his lap.

"Yep," I replied and walked to the door.

"Damn, no kiss?" he frowned and held his hands out. I rolled my eyes and strutted over to peck him lightly and quickly.

Don't get me wrong, I loved my baby daddy, but our relationship had gotten boring. Just because I worked as a schoolteacher, did not mean that I didn't like to have fun like the rest of the ladies out here. All Brax and I did was shop and lay up in the house. He never took me on romantic dates, to the club, and most importantly, he wasn't freaky enough. That's why I was so intrigued by Julius. Julius was a boss ass nigga and the king of the city. On top of that, the shit he texts me, told me he was an all-out freak. I wanted a nigga that would have my body trembling even after we were done, and I knew that was Julius.

I patted my baby girl Tracie's back and then switched out of the house and down the stairs. I spotted Lindy's Toyota Avalon and headed over. As soon as I got into the car, smoke slapped me in the face.

"Damn y'all, they gone have smoke there. And shit that's way better than this," I turned my lip up, and fanned that shit out of my face.

"My bad girl, you know this shit is a habit," Shatan chuckled. We were all schoolteachers by day, but full on bad bitches by night.

"Yeah whatever," I smacked my lips as Lindy pulled away from the curb.

"Baby daddy wasn't tripping?" Lindy questioned.

"Yeah he was earlier, but ain't nobody tryna be at home with his boring ass," I rolled my eyes even though she couldn't see me.

"Don't even let him ruin your night, think about your new boo," she replied and snapped her fingers in a Z.

"Speaking of your new boo, I saw him out to dinner with his little family. Had the kids and everything," Shatan said.

"So what?" I spat.

"And he ain't even fucked you yet? Something ain't right," she added.

"Just because he sees me for more than a piece of ass, unlike the niggas you date, does not mean he's still chasing after that wife of his," I damn near hollered.

Shatan always had some shit to say, but never had a man. Shit I had two men, so she needed to hush and take notes.

We pulled up to the Embassy Suites, and I immediately got wet thinking about Julius dicking me down tonight. We exited the car after parking, and waited in the lobby for Julius to text me the room number.

"Got it, let's go," I told my girls and they followed me to the elevator.

"Welcome beautiful," Julius smiled big with his fine ass when he answered the door. He had on a vintage Indiana Hoosiers baseball jersey, light blue jeans, and Retro Jordan 3's.

"Thank you," I blushed and led my girls into the room.

"Oh Julius, this is Shatan and Lindy," I introduced them and he hugged them both.

The three of us inhaled his sexy Clive Christian cologne, and then turned our attention to the other guys in the room.

"Ladies, this is my brother Rashad, and my homies Leese, Dash, Alonzo, Jabari, Luke and Carl," Julius pointed to his friends who all looked like they had money.

"Nice to meet you," Shatan said in a seductive tone.

There were about fifteen pre rolled blunts and plenty of bottles and food. Currently YG's "Bicken Back Bein Bool" was playing over the speakers, giving it a real hood feel. I was so happy I ditched my boring ass man for this.

I sat down next to Julius, as my friends cozied up with the guys he introduced as Leese and Dash.

"So when are we gonna get some alone time?" I whispered into his ear as he sipped his drink.

"I need you to prove yourself first," he smiled and it was so alluring.

"How?" I rubbed my hand over his crotch and he moved it away.

"Show my boys a good time," he said and raised his eyebrow.

"What? Why?" I asked. I was so confused.

"Look, I told you I was looking for a girl that was down for me. If you can't be the life of the party when I need you to, then this ain't gonna work. That's why I ain't rocking with my wife," he spat and sipped his Jack Daniels again.

"No I'm down babe, I just don't know about all that. I mean we haven't even been physical yet, and you want me to get drop my panties for someone else. Don't you wanna be first?" I licked my lips and rubbed his chest. I could feel how hard it was and my clit throbbed.

"First? With you? Now you know that's not possible," he chuckled and smiled at his friend who was taking Lindy to one of the bedrooms. She just met this nigga less than five minutes ago and was already about to let him fuck.

"You know what I mean Julius. First, out of all your friends," I whined.

"I don't even wanna waste my time getting physical with you if you can't even do one simple thing I fucking asked you to do," he growled. It was scary but sexy.

After a couple moments of silence between us, I asked, "Which friends?"

"Two little homies over there," he replied and pointed to them with his glass.

"Okay, but after I clean up I want it to be me and you," I said and then leaned to kiss his lips but he moved away. "Why don't you ever let me kiss you?" I frowned.

"Prove yourself first," he shrugged.

I got up and pulled my dress down since it was rising up. I sauntered over to his friends and smiled. My dress was pure white and short as hell. My long weave was hanging down my back, and my caramel complexion glowed like the sun.

"What are y'all up to?" I cocked my head.

"Chilling," the one named Luke replied.

"Y'all wanna come chill in the other room?" I questioned and they both shot up off the couch.

I grabbed both of their hands, and started to the bedroom that wasn't occupied by Lindy. I looked over my shoulder at Julius and he smirked at me.

"Let's make this quick," I spat as soon as the door closed. The sooner I fucked them, the quicker I would be bouncing on Julius' dick.

"Can we record?" Jabari smiled.

"Nigga-sure," I fake smiled and then dropped my dress to the floor. I would've said no, but why not have some proof for Julius.

Luke sat down, and then unbuckled his pants to release his dick. It was a pretty nice size so I was surprised by this little ass boy. I dropped to my knees, and started slobbing on his rod as he recorded with his cellphone.

"Smile into the camera for me," Luke panted. I looked up into the phone camera and put extras on my blowjob. "Fuck," Luke moaned as I started to play with his balls.

I continued to slob on his dick as he filmed me. When I'd had enough, I stood up and unbuckled Jabari's pants. Jabari was sexy as fuck. He had smooth chocolate skin, and pretty brown eyes. I kind of wanted to suck and fuck him anyway. Once his pants dropped, I got on my knees and began working my jaws. I felt Luke come behind me, lift my dress and pull my panties to my knees. I pulled Jabari's dick out of my mouth to make sure Luke was strapping up and when I saw he was I went back to pleasing.

"Damn girl," Jabari exhaled as he massaged my scalp with his rough hands.

"Ohh," I purred as I felt Luke slide his dick into my walls.

Jabari was now recording me sucking his dick, and Luke fucking me from behind. I took Jabari's balls into my mouth, as I jacked his dick off with my spit.

"Ahhh, uhhh," I cooed feeling an orgasm rising from Luke.

I took Jabari's dick back into my mouth and he began to hump my face in a circular motion. Luke began to pump me faster, and soon enough he and I exploded at the same time. Jabari spilled his seeds down my throat soon after. I spit it into a nearby trashcan and then once I caught my breath I got up.

"That pussy is fire," Luke commented.

"Of course it is," I retorted.

As much as I didn't want to do that at first, Luke's young ass had me cumming long and hard. I would pretend I didn't enjoy it as much for Julius' sake though. I went into the bathroom and cleaned my vagina before slipping my thong back on. I walked out to go get Julius, and I heard Lindy and that Dash nigga still going at it. I rolled my eyes and entered the living area where everyone else was except Julius and his brother Rashad.

"Where is Julius?" I quizzed frantically.

"He left girl," Alonzo replied and smiled as he sipped his drink.

JULIUS

I was preparing to take a shower when my phone buzzed. I picked it up and saw it was a text from Jabari and Luke. I clicked it to see video of Braxton's girl Sonia, sucking and fucking. I smiled to myself. That stupid hoe fell for all the bullshit I'd told her. As I was about to reply, her name popped up on my work phone.

"Hello?" I answered.

"Nigga, where the fuck are you? How dare you have me fuck your homeboys and then leave, when you told me we were gonna spend the night together!" she shouted.

"Whoa, chill out. I had some business to handle a'ight," I said in a low tone as I peeked out to make sure Natalia was still asleep.

I didn't need my wife thinking I was fucking this hoe, when I had jumped through hoops to make sure that I didn't.

"Oh my bad. When are you coming back?" she questioned.

"I ain't coming back tonight. I will see you another time," I replied and quickly disconnected.

I took a long hot shower and then climbed into bed. I cuddled behind Natalia, and rubbed her protruding belly until I fell asleep.

"**J**ulius!" Natalia yelled as she rocked me.

"What? What is the baby coming?" I inquired frantically.

"No silly, it's way too early for that. Rashad keeps calling," she chuckled and then went into the bathroom.

"Hello?" I said into the phone after taking it from her.

"Nigga, someone robbed two of the traps and killed three of the four niggas that worked there," Rashad sighed.

"What? That wasn't anybody but Brax," I fumed.

"Nah bruh, Owen made it and he said the shooter told him Bart sent him," Rashad responded.

"Oh word?" I chuckled. I knew it was only a matter of time before I had to off Bart.

That nigga had no idea where I laid my head, so he tried to get back at me the best way he could. Little did he know, one of my niggas lived, and now I knew just who had come after me. I knew he was expecting me to go straight for Brax but nope, it was over for Bart. It was sad it had to come to this, but all good things must come to an end.

"Natalia, do not leave the house today," I peeked my head into the bathroom just as she was getting into the tub.

"I was gonna go check on the store-"

"No. No you, Winnie and the kids are gonna stay here. Don't answer the door for anybody unless it's River. I don't care what or who they say they are," I ran off.

"What? Why Ju?" she frowned as she pinned her long brown hair into a bun.

"Nat, baby, just take what I say and let that be it aight?" I frowned and she nodded. I walked over to her, and kissed her lips. I slid my tongue into her sweet mouth, and let it dance with hers for a couple moments. "I love you," I said in a low tone.

"I love you more Ju," she whispered in between kisses.

I rushed to the bathroom outside of our room and brushed my teeth before hopping in the shower. I put on a black t-shirt, black jeans, and the black Jordan sweater 7's. I put on my watch, sprayed my cologne, and then grabbed my black Jordan cap.

"Ju, Winnie made waffles with strawberries on top," Natalia chased me down as I was leaving.

"Babe I ca… okay," I was about to decline, but her beautiful smile started to fade.

"Come on," she grinned and grabbed my hand to lead me to the kitchen.

When we walked in, River was leaving with a plate for Natalia's mother. She mean-mugged me, and then skated out. I sat at the bar with my wife and ate breakfast with her and Winnie. I must say, I enjoyed relaxing and eating breakfast with them, but I had business to tend to. As soon as I was finished, I hopped up from the table and Winnie took my empty plate to clean it.

"Julius, when will you be back? I wanna watch the Martin marathon with you tonight," Natalia called out. I knew she really wanted to spend time with me and I needed to meet her halfway. It's not like I liked leaving her at home or being away from her, I just had shit to do.

"Before ten okay?" I cupped her face and kissed her.

"Promise?" she looked up into my eyes.

"I promise baby girl," I smiled and so did she.

Before I had even made it to the car good, I called Rashad to tell him to have everybody at my office to meet. I needed to find out where Bart was and have him taking a dirt nap by tonight, preferably before 10pm.

I got out the car once I reached my office building, and then rushed inside. Not only was I anxious to get at Bart before he did any more damage, but I needed to make it home to my girl by the time I'd promised her. Before I walked into my conference room, I silenced my work phone because Sonia was blowing me the fuck up.

"What up boss?" everyone said simultaneously.

"Sup. Aight look, has Owen given any more info as to what the guys looked like or anything?" I quizzed getting straight to the point.

"He got shot in the eye. All he heard was *Bart sends his love* before the guy walked out," Rashad replied shaking his head.

"Shit, we need to find out where Bart is. I don't even know if he is in this fucking country!" I banged my fist on the table.

"Yeah, he could've orchestrated this shit from Peru," Dash chimed in and everyone nodded.

"If there was some way Owen could remember more. Did he tell you that they were wearing masks?" I asked.

"Nah, he didn't say," Rashad responded.

"This is the thing, if he can't tell us what that nigga looked like or if he was wearing a mask, kill his ass," I gritted.

"What? Why?" Dash inquired.

"Because, that nigga is lying! He should be able to say if the nigga had on a mask. Then if he says he didn't have on one, he should remember the face of a nigga who shot him in the eye," I replied and Dash smiled to let me know he had caught on.

"I'll go talk to him again," Rashad said.

"No, I need you doing something else with me. Jabari and Luke will go talk to him since they know him a little better. He may be more willing to give up that info. If not, y'all know what to do," I said standing up.

"You know I'm with it. By the way, ole girl from the party was fire," Luke bit his lip and nodded.

"Man, get yo' fucking mind out the gutter and put it in the situation at hand," I chuckled and so did the room.

"I'm trying, I'm trying," Luke smiled and put his hands up in mock surrender.

I ended the meeting and then took Rashad with me to check out the rest of the traps, just to make sure they were good and that no suspicious people were lurking. By the time we were done checking traps and getting more info on the niggas Bart had sent, it was 9:30pm. Shit.

"Aight, Jabari says that Owen said the guys were wearing masks, so now what?" Rashad questioned as I pulled up to my office so he could get his whip.

"We have to kidnap Leah Vargas," I smirked.

"Bart's other daughter? You don't think he has relocated her by now?" Rashad asked.

"Oh yeah I'm sure he has, if he's smart. But, I know where she works and I'm gonna have Dash and Leese get her right out of the parking lot and take her to the warehouse.

"I tell you these niggas be underestimating my little bro," Rashad laughed and dapped me up. "You got your vest on?" he patted my chest.

"Yep, I know to wear this shit when I got enemies," I shook my head and he nodded.

"Good, say hello to Nat for me."

"And say what's up to Lucy," I said and he nodded before jogging to his car. I made sure he was in his car safely and pulling out the parking spot before I peeled off.

I parked my car in the garage and looked down at my phone. The time read 9:55pm. I hopped out, locked my car, and ran inside towards the den. I rushed in there and saw Natalia watching the TV with a tear running down her cheek.

"Baby, why are you crying?" I frowned and rubbed her hair.

"I thought you weren't coming," she smiled and wiped her face. I swear when she was pregnant she cried over everything.

"Ma, I told you I would come. I wouldn't promise you if I wasn't sure," I started to kiss her neck.

"I know," she chuckled and wrapped her arms around my neck to hug me.

"Where is Harmony and Jackson?" I questioned as I looked around the room.

"I just put them to bed about ten minutes ago," she replied as I rubbed her belly.

"A'ight, well go get some snacks from the kitchen and I'm gonna change and kiss them goodnight," I said and she got up excitedly.

I went upstairs, changed into some basketball shorts and a t-shirt and then went to kiss my kids. I went back down to the den and Natalia had drinks, some of her cupcakes, popcorn, water, and candy.

"Damn baby, is this for us or just you?" I joked.

"Shut up," she retorted and lifted the blanket for me to sit under it with her. "Remember when we used to do this at your house in Indiana all the time?" she grinned.

"Yeah, I do. That was when we first became boyfriend and girlfriend," I chuckled.

"When you were crazy as hell. I still loved you though," she said in a low tone as she rubbed my head.

"I don't know how or why you put up with me then, but I'm glad you did," I replied and kissed her cheek.

"Me too," she pecked me and then turned the volume up on the TV a little.

We spent most of the night watching Martin re-runs and then turned the music on to slow dance. I don't know why we liked to do that shit. I remember she asked me to do it one day and ever since then we would do it occasionally. We took a hot bath together, drinking Welch's sparkling drink since she was pregnant, then made love until it was 4am. I always enjoyed the simple things with her.

NATALIA

I was lying in my bed and heard hissing. I tapped next to me, and then sighed when I felt the empty space. Julius had run his ass off somewhere. The hissing sound became even louder, so my eyes shot open. I looked down and there was a snake crawling across me on the bed.

"Ahhhhh!" I screamed and shook my comforter to get it off.

"Eddie, what are you doing in here," River barged in and picked the snake up.

"River, what is that?" I asked.

"My pet snake Eddie," she smiled.

"No, I mean why is he here? With you? At work?" I wiped my eyes.

"He had a cold and I didn't want to leave him home alone," she poked her bottom lip out. She was definitely a basket case.

"River, you have to take that thing home! He could've bitten me," I frowned as I looked over my body to make sure he hadn't already.

"No! He is sick and I will not leave him!" she shouted so loud I jumped. "I-I'm sorry Natalia, I guess I'm just angry still from you breaking my heart," she tucked her lips in and dropped her head.

"River, maybe this arrangement isn't working out anymore. I think you should find a new family to work for," I climbed out of the bed and palmed my stomach.

"No, please Natalia! Don't do that! I need to be with you. If I can't have you, at least let me stay in your presence. Plus, I'm good for your mother," she smiled.

"Stop talking like that! We were not in some relationship River! We had a couple encounters, if you can even call it that!" I furrowed my brows.

"Your mother will die if you get rid of me," she gritted and then walked out.

"Get rid of the snake!" I called after her and she nodded.

I went back into my room and locked the door. I pulled my phone out and called the agency that we hired River from.

"Charleston In-Home Nurse Agency, this is Cathy how may I help you?" a lady sang into the phone.

I walked into the bathroom within my room and closed the door. I sat on the closed toilet top before speaking.

"Yes, hi Cathy. My name is Natalia Tate and I was wondering if I could get a new nurse for my mother," I said.

"Good morning Mrs. Tate. So you're not satisfied with the nurse you have?" she inquired.

"Yes that is correct."

"Okay. Now is this nurse one of ours, or someone you went and hired on your own?" she asked.

"No, she is one of yours. Her name is River York," I sighed.

"River York, let's see," she said. "Oh yes, I see she works for a Julius and Natalia Tate. All right and what is the problem? We don't tell the nurses, it's just so we know what she may need to work on."

"She is...weird, for lack of a better word," I chuckled nervously.

"Weird? Mrs. Tate could you elaborate a little?" she said.

"She brought her pet snake to work and it ended up in my bed," I replied.

"Oh! I'm sorry about that Mrs. Tate. I can have someone come tomorrow morning. Is that okay? You can send her home for the day, and we will break the news to her," she offered.

"Yes please send someone else tomorrow. I'm gonna keep her for the rest of the day though, just because I need the help," I said.

"All right, I will send the new nurse's information to the email listed on file," she stated.

"Thank you."

I prayed that River didn't do anything crazy once she found out that she'd been terminated. I couldn't risk her putting any more animals in my bed, and them harming me and my unborn child.

After my shower, Lucy came to pick me up so that we could go out to eat. We hadn't spent that much time together because of all the work I had to do at the bakery. I had so much to tell her and she just finished cosmetology school, so there was plenty to talk about.

"I've missed you," Lucy smiled as we sat down at High Cotton for brunch.

"I know and I have so much to tell you," I rolled my eyes playfully.

"Me too, but you go first," she smiled.

"Can I get you guys something to drink?" a pretty waitress came to the table.

"Just water for the both of us," Lucy told her.

"Okay, and are you ready to order?" she asked.

"I will have the eggs benedict with a side of apple chicken sausage links," I replied.

"Oooh, I will have the same," Lucy smiled.

"That will be out shortly," the waitress smiled and then walked away.

"Okay, spill please," Lucy chuckled.

"Well I never told you, but Julius caught River going down on me," I clenched my teeth, waiting for her reaction.

"Bitch, what the fuck? So what, were y'all doing that shit on a daily now?" she squinted her eyes.

"No, I told you about the first time. The second time she caught me off guard in the kitchen. The last time she crept into the laundry room and damn near begged me. Julius had been gone for three days, and I was so horny," I laughed and so did she.

"So you used her?" she giggled.

"I hate to say that but, yes. I haven't let her since we got caught though. When Julius caught us, he packed his shit and stormed out. I was grabbing and pulling on him as he walked to the door because I thought he was gonna go sleep with some hoe," I shook my head.

"I'm sure he did," Lucy rolled her eyes.

"Nope! He hasn't cheated in I don't know how long," I cheesed.

"Wow. Who knew little old Natalia could change the big bad wolf, also known as Julius," Lucy joked.

"All it takes is some phenomenal sex, great cooking, cupcakes and unconditional love," I winked as the waiter set the plates down. "So what's the update on you and Rashad?" I asked as I put a forkful of the eggs benedict into my mouth.

"Well," she went into her purse and then pulled her hand out to show a diamond ring. "He asked me to marry him!" she squealed.

"What? Why didn't you tell me?" I grinned.

"Because, I wanted to tell you in person so I could ask you to be my maid of honor," she bit her sausage.

"Of course. I will be better at helping you once I have this baby though." I sighed.

"What is it?" she quizzed.

"We find out next week," I nodded and so did she.

After we ate, we went to shop for a couple of baby things and then we went to my house to relax. We walked into the house around 4:55pm and I hoped River was getting ready to leave.

"You want some tea?" I asked Lucy.

"Yes, I can take some," she replied and followed me to the kitchen. "Is she still here?" she whispered to me as she sat at the bar.

"Yeah, today's her last day though," I whispered back as I started on the tea.

"I will see you tomorrow Natalia. Bye Lucy," River smirked and then floated out of the kitchen.

Lucy turned to me and raised both eyebrows while shaking her head. "That bitch crazy," she said and we burst into laughter.

JULIUS

Tonight we were gonna kidnap Leah Vargas, Bart's other daughter. This was the only way that we could get Bart to come out of hiding so that we could get his ass. Initially we were gonna snatch her ass up from work, but it was still too light outside when she got off. I didn't want to risk anyone seeing us kidnapping her, because that would open a whole new can of worms. So, I had Dash and Jabari follow her home, where they would break in and get her. Once they had her, she would be brought to me.

"Jabari said they're on their way," Rashad said as we sat inside my warehouse.

"They got out of there with no problems, good," I nodded and took a pull on the blunt before handing it to Rashad.

"Sure did, and they should be here in about twenty minutes," Rashad added as he blew out smoke.

"So, Natalia told me you proposed to Lucy," I smiled.

"Yeah, I didn't expect to. It just kind of happened," he chuckled.

"Elaborate because you're not making any sense," I frowned.

"I had Harold, our jeweler, come by the crib so Lucy could pick out something nice. He assumed I was proposing so he brought some iced out ass engagement rings too. Lucy was all over one of them and I just asked her right there in front of Harold," he grinned and passed me back the blunt.

"Wait, so you for real wanna get married or were you just caught up in the moment?" I questioned.

"Both. I loved seeing her smile like that and something just came over me so I asked. Plus, I wanna adopt her son and I think we have to be married for that, I ain't really sure though," he shrugged.

"Wow, weren't you the same nigga saying you would never get married or have kids?" I raised a brow.

"Nigga you shouldn't really be talking. I remember when you wouldn't fuck with a bitch for more than two days and now you're married with damn near three kids," he shook his head and I laughed.

"Yeah, I guess it's true when they say the right woman can change a nigga," I replied as I stared off into the distance.

"Ain't that the truth," Rashad ashed the blunt just as Jabari text him that they'd arrived with Leah.

"MMMMM!" Leah yelled under the sack that was placed over her head. Dash was bringing her in, with Jabari not too far behind.

Rashad and I stood up, and I snatched the bag off her head once they got closer. Her eyes bucked and then squinted as her mind tried to process what the hell was taking place.

"Hi Leah, I'm sorry I had to drag you into this, but your father is to blame," I said as she just stared at me in confusion.

Dash slammed her down into the chair I was originally sitting in, and Rashad started to wrap a rope around her body. She squirmed a little, but Dash was too strong for her. I pulled my work phone out to take a picture of her, and saw I had five text messages from Sonia's thirsty ass. I ignored them and began to snap pictures to send over to Bart.

Me: Come get her.

I sent the text to Bart, and then watched as Dash and Jabari carried the chair holding Leah to a backroom. If Bart didn't agree to come here alone, I would threaten to kill Leah. I had to kill her regardless, because there was no way she would keep quiet about me killing her father. I wasn't about to go and kidnap her ass again just to kill her when I could do it now.

As my boys and I headed out, my phone started to ring. I smiled when I saw it was Bart calling.

"Hello?" I sang into the phone as Rashad and I got into my car together.

"You son of a bitch," he chuckled. It wasn't a funny joke chuckle, it was an angry one. He was furious and I had him right where I wanted him.

"Let her go, she has nothing to do with this," he spat.

"I will let her go when you agree to meet me alone," I said.

"Meet for what? You killed my princess and now you and I are enemies! There is no reason for us to meet!" he shouted.

"Lower your voice Bart. I'm not about to give you an oral presentation on why we should meet. If you don't want your other princess to be dead, you'll quit being a bitch and come step to me," I replied.

It was quiet for a few moments, until he finally asked, "When?"

"How about Thursday night at 10pm? And come alone or you'll regret it. I will be waiting for you with a 9mm pressed to your baby girl's temple. If I see anyone with you, I'm pulling the trigger," I spat and disconnected.

"That nigga is hot! I know he is! I could see the steam coming out of your ear piece!" Rashad joked and we laughed.

"You know he is. I hate to leave his wife a childless widow, but she has her daughter to blame. If Skylar would've just done her job instead of chasing after dick, there would be no problems," I huffed as I made a left turn.

"I know that's right. They brought this shit on themselves," Rashad scoffed.

"And can you believe he hooked up with that nigga Brax? I should've known he'd do something like that, because he did it to Hugo," I frowned.

"Speaking of Brax, you send him that video yet?" Rashad grinned.

"Nah, I have to get his email out of Natalia's computer. But when I do, I'll have it in his inbox in no time," I cheesed and dapped my brother up.

"When he sees that shit, he's gonna go ape shit dawg," Rashad snickered.

"And that's exactly what the fuck I want him to do. Soon as he gets to barking, I'm gone put some heat in him," I smiled more so to myself.

"Then we need to go on a vacation to celebrate the end of all these snake niggas," Rashad exhaled and I nodded in agreement.

I dropped Rashad off and then went home. It was around 12am and I knew Natalia would be asleep. This was the perfect time for me to go into her computer and get Brax's email. I would shoot that shit over to him from a throwaway email I created and then sit back and watch for the explosion.

I crept into the house and the lights were slightly dim all over. I went into the kitchen first, and checked the fridge for a plate of food. I smiled when I saw a plate of yams, fried chicken, and creamed spinach. For dessert, there was a chocolate chip cheesecake. I licked my lips because I knew getting that email was gonna have to wait until after I ate. Good thing I worked out, because at the times I was eating, I was bound to get fat if I didn't.

I scarfed down my dinner and cheesecake, then showered and brushed my teeth. I turned my iPhone's flashlight on and searched the bedroom quietly for Natalia's laptop.

"Julius what are you doing?" Natalia scared the shit out of me.

"Oh, umm, I dropped my earring babe," I lied.

"Turn the light on," she whispered.

"Nah, it's cool. Go back to sleep," I said.

"Come lay with me. I need you to rub my tummy," she chuckled. Shit.

"A'ight," I sighed and went to lay down with her. I knew she wouldn't take no for an answer and I couldn't risk her finding out what I was doing.

I couldn't sleep at all throughout the night, because all I could think about was getting that damn email. It worked in my favor though, because when Natalia got up to shower, it woke me up out of the light slumber I'd drifted off to.

I looked over my shoulder and saw her go into the bathroom within our room. As soon as the door closed, I rolled over and off the bed like a damn '007' agent. Since it was morning time, it was much easier to see. I spotted her laptop bag by her vanity and rushed over to open it. I pulled it out and pressed the power button. My leg bounced nervously as I waited for her MacBook to boot up. *Come on, come on*, I chanted in my head as I listened to the shower water. Once it was up and on, I clicked her email app and quickly typed Brax into the search box.

"Braxton@NorthlandPR.com," I read it off out loud, as I typed it into my phone.

I double checked it and then powered her computer off. What the fuck was this nigga doing in the public relations business? I shook my head at his double life and then put her laptop back into her bag. I pulled my gloves from my black duffle bag and slid them on. I grabbed Leah's phone that we'd taken from her and saved the video that Jabari had sent to it. I sent the video to Brax's email from my dummy email that I'd added onto Leah's phone.

"Julius-" Natalia came out of the bathroom and since my nerves were on edge, the phone flew up out of my hands and hit the ceiling. "Ju, are you okay? Why are you wearing gloves?" she frowned.

"I always wear gloves when I use my work phone babe," I chuckled nervously.

"Oh okay," she smirked and leaned her head back for a kiss.

I picked the phone up off the floor and finished what I was doing. I took the phone to the backyard and then burned it. Thank God Leah lived in the same vicinity as me, so her phone would show up as using the same cell phone towers that she always used. I didn't want there to be any suspicions.

NATALIA

THAT AFTERNOON

I was in the back putting orders on my calendar, because so many were coming in and I needed to keep track. It was bittersweet though, because I was making a lot of money, yet I was working extra hard. I think because I was pregnant, I was always more tired than I usually would've been after only a little amount of work.

"Where is the fucking manager?" I heard someone yell from the front.

"Nat, we have a problem," my employee Brittani peeped her head into my office, just as I was standing up.

"I can hear that. I'm coming," I chuckled and followed her to the front.

I walked out and it was some light-skinned chick yelling at the top of her lungs at my employee Casey. I couldn't even understand what she was saying because her annoying voice was so high pitched.

"Can I help you?" I frowned. I wasn't in the mood for this. My back was hurting, my feet were swollen and I was hungry and horny.

"Uh, who are you?" she asked with a smirk.

"I'm Natalia, the executive pastry chef and owner," I replied.

"Natalia, yes. I wanted to take advantage of the 'buy three get two free' promotion here, but your employee won't allow it," she placed her hand on her thick hip. She reminded me of Erica Mena from *Love and Hip Hop.*

"I see. Which cupcakes were you looking to get?" I inquired as Casey and Brittani looked on.

"I wanted five of the lemon rosemary and smoked salmon cupcakes," she raised a brow.

"So the savory cupcakes are not a part of the promotion like it says here," I told her and pointed to the sign.

"That is some bullshit! It's always a catch with these fucking promotions!" she yelled.

"Let's lower our voices ma'am-"

"Do I look old enough to be a ma'am Natalia? Call me Sonia," she cut me off to say.

"Sonia, please lower your voice and can you step to the side so my employee can help the people behind you," I said before we walked to the side. "Now, unfortunately the smoked salmon cupcakes are not a part of the promotion, but I will be happy to honor it with any of our non-savories," I half-smiled once we were away from the small crowd.

She stared at me for a second and folded her arms. "Aren't you married to Julius?" she cheesed.

"Umm, yes I am," I squinted my eyes. "Now which-"

"Has he asked you for a divorce yet?" she inquired.

"Why is my personal life your business? I must've missed a few portions of the conversation, because I'm not sure how we got here," I folded my arms like her.

"See, Julius and I are very much in love, and he told me he was gonna ask you for a divorce very soon. He's slow poking around, so I thought I'd get the ball rolling for him. I know it's hard for him to tell you such a devastating thing when you're pregnant with his child," she gave me a fake sympathetic expression.

"Wait, what the fuck are you talking about? I don't have time to entertain groupies okay," I put my hand up.

"You want proof wife?" she offered.

"Sure, humor me," I chuckled. I knew this hoe was lying. Julius wouldn't dare cheat on me. He hadn't done so in forever and I knew he had no plans on doing so now.

"There you go. Scroll up," she handed me her iPhone.

The number was stored as My Love. I scrolled through the texts, and my stomach started to feel queasy as I read the things he said. It was mostly sexual and very inappropriate for him to be texting her in this way. It was obvious she was a booty call type, but I didn't give a fuck. I was furious.

"Here you go. Like I said, savories aren't a part of the deal. Have a good day," I smiled and handed her the phone back.

I went to my office and grabbed my coat and purse. I knew Julius was at home, so he was about to get an earful and then get the fuck out. I made sure not to speed, because I didn't want my anger to end up killing my baby or me. I drove into our garage once I got home and then walked slowly into the house to give myself time to calm down. I arrived at Julius' office door and knocked lightly.

"Come in," he called out. "Hey sexy, I thought you were gonna be at the bakery until five," he smiled with his fine self.

"I'm sure you wished I did stay until five so that you could have some alone time with Sonia," I raised a brow as I closed the door behind me. His face immediately dropped.

"Natalia I can explain-"

"Explain what Ju? This is over. I can only take so much! It isn't possible for you to love me because you have no regard for my feelings! Ever!" I started to cry. Fuck! I didn't want to cry right now but these damn hormones got the best of me.

"Natalia, sit down babe and let me explain," he pulled a chair out for me.

"Explain how she came up in my bakery causing a fucking scene! Then she whips out her phone and shows me all the freaky shit you were texting her! And the bonus was the fact that she had you stored as My Love!" I hollered.

"How did you even know it was me if she didn't have me stored under my name? Did you even look at the number?" he questioned and smiled at the thought of him being able to wiggle his way out of this.

"I didn't need to verify the number dummy. I've been with you long enough to know what you text like!" I spat.

"A'ight, I'm gonna come clean Nat," he sighed.

"About time. Hurry up so I can call our lawyer," I folded my arms across my chest.

I had my fists balled up, because as soon as he said something I didn't like, I was gonna fuck him up. I was a far cry from the little sixteen-year old he met in Indiana that he could just do anything to.

"Sonia is Brax's girlfriend. When he started talking to you, it was to fuck with me, so in return I got at his girl. BUT, I didn't sleep with her or anything. I just sent her those things to string her along. It worked and I got her to sleep with my homies to fuck with Brax. Usually if I was single, I would've just got some head from her myself, but because I love you," he smiled nervously. "I went through all this extra shit to have someone else sleep with her," he finished and waited for my response.

WHAM!

I slapped him hard as fuck because I was upset that he was doing all of this bullshit behind my back. If he had have told me, I would've been up on game when that hoe came at me like that.

"Natalia! I swear I'm being honest!" he screeched like a bitch.

"I know, I believe you," I smirked.

"Well then why the fuck did you slap me?" he quizzed while still holding his face.

"Because you should've told me what you were doing!" I stood up and smoothed down my dress. "Now what do you want for dinner so Winnie and I can cook?" I asked trying to keep myself from laughing.

He just stared at me as if I had two heads, because he was still perplexed that I had slapped him like he was a hoe that didn't have my money.

"I'm sorry baby. I didn't mean to hit you that hard," I chuckled and kissed his sore cheek softly. "I think Winnie is making ribs tonight, one of your favorites," I added and pecked his lips softly before sauntering out.

I knew he thought I was crazy but I didn't care. I met Winnie in the kitchen and she passed me the seasoning to start on the ribs. Suddenly, the house phone rang and I saw it was my bakery.

"Hello?" I frowned because it was odd for them to be calling, especially on the house phone.

"Nat, you have to come down here. Someone put a box of snakes in the corner of the store and now they're all over the floor. Latoya has closed the bakery for now and called someone down to get them, but you have to come look at the footage so we can see who did this," my employee Nikki ran off into the phone.

"Snakes? What the hell?" I shook my head. I was the only person that had access to rewinding the cameras, so I had to go down there. "I will be there in a second," I replied and hung up.

I parked right in front of my bakery and power walked in. I locked the door behind me and saw the guys that were capturing the snakes.

"I'm guessing you're Mrs. Tate?" one of the guys said, as Latoya emerged from the back.

"Yes," I nodded as I inspected the floor.

"Nice to meet you. These snakes were definitely someone's pets. They're not your average wild snakes. I don't know if that helps you figure out who it was, but I thought I'd tell you," he pursed his lips and exhaled.

"Thank you," I replied.

"Okay, just sign this work order for me and you're all set. My partner and I caught them all," he handed me a clipboard. I signed it and then let them out.

Latoya and I went to the back and cued up the footage on the TV. We watched closely and I saw a small skinny figure slip in with a small box. Because we were so busy all the time, Casey, Nikki and Brittani didn't even see her; her being River. I knew that skinny frame and that walk that lacked confidence anywhere.

"You know who it is?" Latoya asked.

"Absolutely," I responded and stood to my feet.

"Who?" she frowned.

"I'll handle it," I said before skipping out.

When I got into my car, I sifted through my emails until I came across the one from the nursing agency containing River's information. I clicked the attached pdf, and scanned it for her home address. I clicked it and then let Siri lead me to the destination. I pulled up to a small cozy home and threw the car in park.

"Who is it?" River called out after I rang the doorbell. "What?" she asked from behind the door. I guess she saw me through her peephole.

"I wanna talk River," I replied.

"Talk about what? You fired me!" she shouted.

"About us. I wanna apologize," before I could even get the words out, the door opened a little.

"You're not mad about the snakes?" she questioned with the chain still on the door.

"No, I deserved that. I shouldn't have done what I did to you. It was wrong to use you," I half-smiled and she blushed.

She closed the door and then removed the chain. "Come in," she grinned.

"Nice," I said as I walked in and admired her place.

"Would you like some hot cocoa?" she quizzed.

"No, let's talk," I smiled.

My plan was to be kind to her so that she would stop fucking with me. I would hate for Julius to have to kill her over something so small. I guess when Julius said I had some gold between my legs, he wasn't joking.

"So what did you wanna talk about Natalia?" she asked as she moved my hair behind my ear.

"I want to call a truce River. I don't wanna be enemies anymore. What I did was wrong and putting snakes in my bakery was wrong. Let's just call it even," I said.

"That's not gonna work for me. I know one way we could call it even though," she bit her lip.

"How? A check?" I wondered.

"Let me do it one more time," she licked her lips.

"Do what one more time?" I played stupid. I prayed she was talking about cleaning the shit stains out of my mother's sheets.

"You know, let me taste you. It's like a drug for me," she said in a low tone as she rubbed my thigh.

"River, I'm five months pregnant. Why would you even want to?" I furrowed my brows.

"You were pregnant when I did it before?" she cheesed.

"Yes, but I wasn't as far along." I chuckled nervously.

She ignored me and got onto the floor. She ran her skinny hands up my thigh until she reached my panties. *If I do this, she will go away*, I thought.

"No, no stop," I pushed her hand away once she started to tug on my panties.

"Come on, you know you want to," she smirked.

"No, no I don't," I pushed her lightly and pulled my dress back down. "Let's just call it even River, please. I just want to move on from this and be with my family," I begged.

"Don't beg, you're turning me on," she laughed.

"River!"

"No! You should've thought about your family before you let me make love to you!" she screamed.

Why did she keep saying that? Since when is one sided oral sex making love? Normally I would've beaten her ass, but I wasn't in the condition to do so.

"I don't want this to get ugly River. I'm giving you one more chance to just let this all go," I panted.

She walked close to my face and whispered, "No."

JULIUS

Bart and Leah were gonna be sweet memories after tonight. Dash, Leese and I were all set up and ready to go. My brother Rashad couldn't come, because tonight he was taking Lucy on some romantic date or some shit. I wasn't tripping because the three of us were more than enough.

"So you want us to come in?" Leese asked as he loaded his gun.

"Nope, I only need y'all to act if y'all see he has people with him. While he's in there with me, if you see any strange persons coming up, just blast their asses," I replied.

"Aight," Leese nodded.

I left Dash and Leese in the car and went inside the warehouse. I made sure I had on my bulletproof vest, in case Bart pulled any bitch moves on me. I entered the room that held Leah and saw she was passed out, snoring and everything. I took bottled water from the floor and doused her with it.

"Ah, what?" she mumbled and shot her eyes open while looking around.

"Ya daddy is on his way," I sighed and she just stared at me.

Just then, my phone buzzed and I pulled it out to see a text from Bart.

B. Vargas: *Coming in.*

Me: *Come straight to the back.*

As I waited for Bart to come to the back, I silenced my gun and made sure everything was in place. While I was preparing myself, Leah looked at me with a worried expression. She tried to talk, but the tape over her mouth hindered her from doing so.

"Princess," Bart exclaimed when he entered the room. Leah began to squirm wildly, as Bart neared her.

PHEW!

PHEW!

Before he could even touch her, I emptied two shots into his head. His eyes bucked and he slumped to the floor right at Leah's feet. I knew I couldn't let him live because he would bring me too many problems. One, he had hooked up and agreed to supply Brax on my territory and two, I knew he would never stop until I was dead because of Skylar.

"MMMM!" Leah screamed and squirmed as tears ran down her face.

I hated to do her like this because she hadn't done anything. I thought of many ways to be able to spare her life but nothing made sense. The fact of the matter is, if I let her go she would go right to the police about her father's murderer.

"I really wanted to keep you alive," I knelt down on the side of her. "Don't scream," I added as I peeled the duct tape off her mouth.

"Please Julius, I won't say anything," she sobbed.

"I don't know you well enough to trust you, ma. I did some bad shit and I see no reason for you not to run off and tell the cops," I replied somberly.

"Ahhhh," she threw her head back as she cried softly. I actually felt bad for her and I didn't know why. "I can go home to Peru," she offered.

"Leah, I'm gonna put you on a plane tonight. I know people there and if I find out you're back here in the states, I will have you killed. Even if I'm in jail, I will have you killed. No matter where you are, or who you're with, I will have you killed," I promised her.

A part of me was saying just kill her, but the other wouldn't allow me to take an innocent life. She hadn't done anything, and was always welcoming to me whenever she saw me.

"Julius I swear on my life I won't give you any problems. My mother is already in Peru and I will make up a reason as to why daddy isn't coming back," she sniffled.

I didn't say anything as I untied her. She was weak so I carried her bridal style out of the warehouse and when Dash and Leese saw me, they exited the car.

"What the-"

"Just go clean up Bart's body," I cut Leese off. He and Dash took their duffle bags inside without another word.

I put Leah in the car and then sat in the backseat with her. It was quiet for a few moments, as we just waited for Dash and Leese to come out. While waiting, I texted my pilot along with Luke and Jabari so they could accompany her on the flight tonight.

"Thank you," Leah kissed my cheek.

"I don't know if you're welcome yet," I chuckled.

"You won't regret this Julius. I know this is all Skylar's fault. You did what you had to do to protect your business. It's not only commendable, but very attractive," she turned my face to look into her eyes.

"Thanks," I responded and moved my face away.

"A'ight, where the fuck are we taking her?" Dash asked as he slid into the driver seat.

"Gavin is gonna fly her to Peru tonight. Jabari and Luke should be there to escort her when we get to the port," I said and he nodded before cranking the car.

By the time I got home, it was 3am. I was extremely exhausted yet still stressed. I'd gotten rid of Bart and hopefully Leah, but Brax was still gonna be a problem. I knew it was only a matter of time before he checked his email and saw that video. Once he did, he would wreak havoc and I was prepared to take his ass down.

After I took a shower in the downstairs bathroom, I went to the kitchen to grab a bottle of water. I downed it, and then put it in the recycle bin before running up the stairs quietly. I slipped into my kids' rooms and kissed their cheeks lightly. I really needed to make sure I took some time off, because I felt like I wasn't being a good father. I didn't have one and I wanted to make sure my kids saw a healthy marriage and even better parents.

I walked into Natalia and my bedroom, to see Natalia lying in the middle of the bed. She had on a little bra and no underwear, I guess because it was really hot during this time. My dick sprang up and an evil smile spread across my face. I slowly neared her and stepped out of my boxers. I spread her legs to view her pretty pussy and then dropped to my knees to take her clit into my mouth. She tasted so sweet, that I just closed my eyes to savor the moment.

"Ju..." she whispered as she came to.

I pulled her to the edge of the bed so that I could have more access and continued to attack. I darted my tongue into her hole and then trailed it back up to her clit before sucking it gently again. I kept doing that until her juices came flowing into my mouth. I stood up and then put her back into the middle of the bed.

"Be gentle," she said in a low tone.

I lowered myself close to her, until her hard belly poked my abs. I kissed her sweet soft lips and slowly wiggled my way inside her. The feeling was indescribable, just like always. Ever since the first time I fucked her, I always had to coach myself so I wouldn't cum immediately.

"Damn Nat," I mumbled as I slowly thrust into her tight, wet, warm, walls.

She put her small hands on my biceps and ran them up and down, digging in her nails every now and then. I pulled her bottom lip into my mouth, as I pumped her in a circular motion.

"I love you Julius," she threw her head back and I pulled her bra strap down to expose her small, round, plump, breasts.

I took one of her nipples into my mouth and sucked them hungrily. She caressed the back of my head, as soft whimpers escaped her mouth. I pecked her belly one time and then lifted my head to kiss her passionately again.

"Soon as you have our baby, I'm gonna fuck you nice and hard," I smirked and so did she.

"I can't- uuhhhh- wait," she moaned.

I sped up a little, making sure not to go too fast, until the both of us came hard. We were sweating so hard that it looked like we had just come out of a pool. I fell to the side of her and she cuddled up next to me until we fell asleep.

BRAXTON

"Fuck, damn bitch," I groaned as I fucked Natalia's little employee Nikki.

I gripped her small waist and plowed into her ass hard. Her fat ass was jiggling all over the place and I knew I'd be cumming any minute now.

"Ooooh," she called out as she released her juices.

"Errgghhh," I growled as I filled up the condom. I jerked slightly and then slid out slowly to go flush the condom.

I came from the bathroom and Nikki was lying down with the sheet over her sexy body. I climbed in next to her, and she laid her head on my chest. I grabbed my phone to see if I had any messages from Sonia or Bart. I hadn't talked to either of them in a couple days and I was starting to become irritated. I called my phone service provider to make sure my shit was on, because it wasn't like Bart not to respond. Sonia was flat out ignoring me and she had my daughter wherever she was. A couple people told me they'd seen her out, so I knew she wasn't lying dead anywhere.

"You okay?" Nikki asked.

"Yeah, I'm good. What time do you have to be at work?" I questioned because I was ready for her to go. Not because I didn't like her, but because I needed to handle some business.

"I have to be there at 6am," she pouted.

"Damn, maybe you should go home and get some rest," I suggested.

"Why? It's only 7pm, and I was thinking I could spend the night," she smiled.

"Uh, you can spend the night when you don't have work in the am," I replied half-smiling and she plopped her head back onto the pillow.

Speaking of Natalia, I needed to check my email and see if she had finally responded to what I'd sent her. She didn't say anything the initial day I sent it, but I assumed it was because Julius was in the way. I sat at my computer as Nikki flipped through the TV channels, and opened my email. I had a message from a weird ass email address. I wasn't gonna click it, but then again the email address *Come Get Ya Bitch at gmail dot com* had me intrigued. I opened it and clicked on the video attached. What I saw made my heart drop and my stomach bubble.

The woman I had given my all to and loved more than anything, was getting a train ran on her by some niggas that looked fresh out of the womb. Sonia had the game fucked up, and I was about to find her ass. Hopefully, I didn't murder her, because I would hate to take my daughter Tracie's mother away from her.

I pulled out my phone, and dialed her number just to see if she would answer. I waited impatiently for her to pick up, but only got the voicemail. I called one more time, and to my surprise, the bitch answered like she hadn't been missing in action this whole time.

"Hey boo," she sang.

"Yo, where the fuck you at Sonia?" I quizzed and immediately remembered Nikki was here. She shot daggers at me and hopped up to get dressed.

"I'm doing my thing Brax. We need some time apart," she exhaled. I rushed over to Nikki, and sat her down so that she wouldn't leave.

"Let me come talk to you for a second. Where are you?"

"My mothers. Hurry the fuck up though because I got-"

I hung up on her ass, and tended to a furious Nikki.

"Move Brax, I knew you wasn't about shit," Nikki frowned as she tried to release herself from my embrace.

"Look, she's just my baby mama. I'm only trying to track her down so that I can see my daughter. I haven't seen my baby in three damn days," I pleaded. "Just stay here and spend the night with me," I smiled and she did too.

"Fine Brax, but don't be gone long," she replied and began to remove her shoes.

"I won't. Don't leave," I kissed her lips and then quickly got dressed.

I could kill Sonia right now. I wasn't sure if I was more upset that she had just dipped on me with my daughter, or that she was around here getting ran through like some common hoe. It made me wonder what the fuck she was doing during my seven years in the pen.

I parked in front of her mama's house, and braced myself before knocking on the door. I heard my daughter's voice, and a smile crept across my face. Finally, the door opened, and Sonia's sexy ass stood behind it.

"Hello to you too," I spat and then focused my attention on my kid.

"Daddy!" she squealed and ran towards me.

"I missed you," I whispered as I hugged her tightly. "Can you go to the back with grandma so I can chat with mommy for a bit?" I grinned.

"For ten dollars," she replied holding out her little hand. She was like her mama already.

"Scam artist," I joked at slapped a ten-dollar bill into her hand. Once she ran off to her grandmother's room, I diverted my attention back to Sonia.

"Make this quick," she twisted her face up.

"Sonia, what the fuck is going baby? You out here getting trains ran on you?" I frowned and sat next to her on the couch. I was hurt, disappointed, disgusted, angry, and a whole bunch of other shit.

"What are you talking about?" she rolled her eyes.

"This," I retrieved my phone from my pocket, and showed her the video.

"Oh that," she chuckled and handed it back. "Look Brax, you and I ain't gonna work no more. I've moved on and I'm happy," she stated as if she was just telling me what she cooked for dinner.

"What? You my muthafuckin' girl! Who the fuck could you have possibly hooked up with that's got you ready to move on like that?" I asked.

"Julius Tate," she smiled and giggled like she was so happy. The sound of his name made my skin crawl.

"Julius Tate? That nigga has a wife, two kids, and a damn baby on the way. What the fuck is you talking about Sonia?" I was more confused than ever. I knew I should have been more aggressive in pursuing Natalia.

"Yeah, yeah, yeah. He's divorcing her, and him, Tracie and me are gonna be a family. I did that train for him. It was to show him I'm the real deal," she nodded.

"The real deal? If you're the real deal, then why he got you here with ya mama, but has his wife at home with him?" I raised a brow. How dumb could she be? She had a college degree, yet allowed some young nigga to talk her into a train.

"You know nothing of what you speak Braxton. Just know that you and I are a wrap!" she shouted in my face and ran her hand across her neck to signal chopping.

"You ain't taking my fucking daughter, and becoming a family with no damn body!" I yelled.

"Tracie ain't ya fucking baby! Damn! Billy is her daddy!" she boomed.

"My fucking cousin?" I stared at her as if she had shit growing out of her face.

"Yes! I fucked him because you were always in the streets and leaving me at home! Plus, I knew you were fucking all kinds of other bitches. Billy comforted me, and would tell me every time you cheated on me. One night we fucked, and from there it never stopped," she explained and then exhaled. "That felt good. I hated harboring that shit," she chuckled to herself.

"Sonia, tell me you just fucking with me," I said in a low tone.

"I wish I was. Billy wanted a DNA test and we got it. It came back that he was the father, but we both agreed to lie," she shrugged. She shrugged like it was nothing.

I was mad at too many people right now and I didn't know what to do. I wanted to strangle Sonia for doing me dirtier than anybody in this fucking world. But, I wanted to blast Billy for betraying me in the worst way. That nigga was like my brother, and not only did he go behind my back and tell of my infidelities, but he smashed my girl and got her pregnant. The other nigga on my hit list was Julius. He really hit me where it hurt by having the woman I love act like a common hood rat. A train? Really Julius? Yeah, I was wrong for coming for his wife first but damn! Then it was Bart, where the fuck was he? We were supposed to discuss a shipment schedule to be put in motion, and now this nigga was ghost. I was in over my head right now.

"I can't believe this shit," I finally said as I rubbed my eyes.

"Well believe it be-"

WHAM!

I slapped the shit out of her, and blood spewed from her nose.

WHAM!

WHAM!

I slapped her two more times, and she screamed and cowered on the floor. I stood up off the couch and panted over her, as her mother came from the back.

"Get out Braxton! What the hell is wrong with you?" her mother shouted as she crouched down to tend to Sonia's wounds.

I stepped over her, and rushed outside. I was about to put a few niggas in the dirt, and I was starting with Julius. Shit if he was gone, I would benefit in so many ways. I would be able to have his wife, and take back over the area regardless of working with Bart.

As I walked down the walkway to my car, a black sack was placed over my head and I was dragged to the left. I squirmed wildly, and screamed because I had no idea what the fuck was going on. This was not my damn night! I felt myself being thrown in a car, and before I could say anything, I was clocked over the head with something that felt like a gun.

My eyes fluttered as I attempted to adjust them to the light. My head was hanging down, and I could see I was tied to a chair. The floor looked dirty, and I had no idea where I was. I finally got enough strength to pick my head up, and saw two niggas I'd never seen before.

"Morning sunshine," one of them smiled, and ashed his blunt.

My head was throbbing, and I just didn.t feel good enough to say anything. I watched as the other guy stood up, and then exited the room. I shut my eyes, and took a couple deep breaths in order to collect my thoughts. The door of the room opened, and in walked the last nigga I wanted to see while being tied up with a busted head, Julius.

"What's up homie?" he grinned. I simply smacked my lips and looked away. "Oh, you a mute now?" he cocked his head and folded his arms. "I gave you chance to get down with the team, but you just had to go against me," he shook his head and pulled a chair up.

"Nigga, I'm way older than you, and been doing this shit way longer! You need to be working for me!" I hollered.

"Feisty," one of the guys laughed.

"Well, do you have any last words Brax?" Julius raised a brow as he pulled his gun from his waist.

I couldn't believe that this twenty-three-year-old nigga had fucked me over like this. He had my bitch gone in the head over him, made my connect disappear, and now had me tied up in some random room about to put a bullet in me.

"I give you your props Mr. Julius, you're a for real thug ass nigga; a hood king. If I were younger, I would have no problem working for you. But with the track record I have, and with all the work I've put in, I just can't go out like that," I said.

"It ain't about age, it's about who works and moves smarter, and clearly that person is me. You should have no problem working for me, because I have forgotten more rules to the game than you even have in your brain right now. I ain't no little ass wanna be dope boy trying to play king of the streets. Too bad you couldn't recognize that earlier, because we could've made a lot of money together. But once you start to dip into my family life, it gets you an automatic hollow tip," he replied and I nodded.

He was right, but like he said, it was too late to make amends now. We both had gone too far to forgive one another, more so him than me. I did nothing to harm Natalia, but any hustler in the game knew when you even spoke to another hustler's girl, wife, or baby mama, all bets were off.

I looked down, and then looked back up to stare him in the eyes. He cocked his gun, and then let off two shots between my eyes.

NATALIA

Harmony's Bake Shoppe had been making a lot of money. We were selling so many cupcakes, that I had to hire two extra pastry chefs to help me bake. I loved that I had my own money and it had nothing to do with Julius. He didn't mind giving me money, but I still wanted to have my own because you never know how things can turn out. I doubt we'd ever break up though.

I turned in the store deposit to the bank, and then texted Lucy to let her know she could meet me at my house. As I was walking to my car, I noticed it was much shorter than usual. I looked down at the tires, and realized I was sitting on four flats. I didn't need to question because I knew this was River's doing. I pulled my phone from my purse, and called Julius before anybody else. I tried to spare River but she was asking for it.

"Hey beautiful," Julius answered and made me feel warm inside. No matter how many times he answered the phone that way, it still made me feel fuzzy all over.

"Julius, she flattened my tires," I whined.

"Who?" he asked.

"River! She won't leave me alone! I didn't tell you, but she put snakes in my bakery. She told me she won't leave me alone unless I let her do what she did again," I explained.

"Wow a'ight. Call AAA and I'm gonna come get you. Where are you?" he questioned.

"I'm at the Bank of America on Sam Rittenberg Boulevard," I sighed.

"A'ight," he disconnected the call, and then I called for a tow.

***

"That bitch did what?" Lucy exclaimed. We were sitting in the den eating chicken pasta and watching TV, while Rashad and Julius played video games in the other den.

"She flattened my fucking tires! All four of them," I frowned and shoved some food into my mouth.

"Damn, that bitch must be Hercules, because popping tires is hard as fuck," Lucy bucked her eyes.

"How the fuck do you know?" I chuckled.

"I've done my share of crazy shit in the past," she winked and I shook my head. "So, what now?"

"Julius said he will take care of it tomorrow when I take the babies to the doctor. He wants me gone and to have an alibi if anything happens," I replied.

"Okay Mrs. Tate, I am leaving for the day," the new nurse Reese peeked her head into the den.

"Alright, see you in two days," I smiled and she nodded.

"In two days?" Lucy frowned.

"Yes, we give her one weekday off in order for her to come in on Saturday. Just because Winnie and I are really busy on Saturdays," I responded.

Suddenly, Rashad and Julius entered the den, laughing and talking loud as fuck. They sat down next to us, and Rashad immediately started kissing Lucy. I hadn't seen him this happy with a girl since he first met Paula. Julius rubbed my belly as I polished off my chicken pasta.

"Natalia! It's your mother! I've called 911!" Winnie shouted running into the den.

"What? What happened?" I asked as I got up off the couch.

"I think she had a heart attack!" Winnie panicked.

"Relax Winnie!" Julius replied and rushed out.

We heard sirens outside the house, and I was glad that they came quick. Tears started to flow, because for some reason, I knew my mother was gone. She had been so sick, and she didn't seem to be getting any better.

Winnie let the EMT's in, and they quickly placed my mom on the stretcher and rushed her out. Lucy, Rashad, Julius, and I, piled into Julius' car to follow. Winnie stayed home to tend to Jackson and Harmony.

As soon as we arrived to the hospital, Julius parked quickly and we all hopped out. I was crying non-stop, and my heart was beating fast.

"Calm down Nat, you're pregnant," Lucy rubbed my back as we all walked into the hospital.

Through tears, I could see them rushing my mom to the back. She was passed out, and I had no idea what was gonna happen with her. The four of us sat down, and I prayed for her to be okay. Although she wasn't the greatest mother, I needed her to be okay.

We waited for about twenty minutes, before someone came out looking for the family of Dalia Gaines. Julius got up to help me stand to my feet, and then we neared the doctor. I hoped we got the same news from when Lucy was in a similar situation.

"Who are you to Ms. Gaines?" the doctor asked.

"I-I'm her daughter, Natalia Tate. Th-Thomas is my maiden name," I stammered. *Please say something good. Please say something good*, I chanted in my head.

"Ms. Tate, I'm sorry but all attempts to resuscitate your mother were unsuccessful. I-" the doctor replied and I heard nothing else of what he spoke.

Was this really happening or was this a dream? We weren't close, but I loved her just as much as any child loved their mother. I loved her even though she didn't love me.

"Natalia!" Julius snapped me back to reality.

"Nooo," I immediately broke down in tears. Julius held me up because I couldn't do it myself.

"I'm very sorry Ms. Tate. Would you like to come to the back with the pastor and pray over your mother?" the doctor asked. I simply nodded, and Julius waved Rashad and Lucy to come with us.

We followed the doctor to my mother's room, and as soon as I saw her, I began to cry again. Lucy was sniffling lightly as she looked on as well. I cried into Julius' chest as the pastor prayed over my mother. I said a few words through tears, and then the four of us left to go home.

"Winnie made you some hot chocolate," Julius handed me a mug.

"Thanks," I whispered.

"I know you're sad about your mother babe, but if you need anything, know that I'm here for you a'ight?" Julius said as he climbed into the bed.

"She was only thirty-five," I said in a low tone.

"It's unfortunate, but be happy that she isn't suffering anymore. She's finally at peace," he rubbed my back.

I downed the hot chocolate, and then turned the lamp off. I felt the tears coming up as I laid on Julius' chest. He held me as I cried hysterically until I fell asleep. He put his plans for River on hold, as well as his work for a couple weeks, to be by me until I felt a little better.

I hadn't heard from Natalia since the snake incident. I had slashed her tires in the bank parking lot, and still got nothing. Did she think I was kidding? There was no way she was gonna get away with using me.

However, today my prayers were answered. I took a midday nap, and woke up to a text from her saying to come over. I was gonna bring my gun because I wanted to make her comply with anything that I told her. My mouth was watering at the thought of tasting her again, and maybe I could get her to do me this time too.

I slipped into a tight black dress for easy access, and then black stilettos to match. I frowned in the mirror because I hated my skinny frame. I had A-cup breasts, and no ass to match. I was shaped just like a damn surfboard. I wished I looked like Natalia though. She was average height, 5'5, with a small yet shapely frame. She was slim thick, not too much but just enough. My clit jumped at the thought of her, so I grabbed my purse and keys, and then rushed out.

I parked my car down the street, and then went to type in the code to their gate. It buzzed letting me know that I had typed in the wrong numbers. *They changed it*, I thought. I pressed the button so Natalia could let me in.

"Hello?" her sweet voice came through the box.

"Hey baby I'm here. Let me in," I smirked.

The smaller gate buzzed, and I twisted the knob to go in. I hiked up their long roundabout driveway, and finally reached the door. I panted for a little bit, then pressed the round doorbell button. I heard the sound of heels, and a smile spread across my face. I couldn't wait to see her sexy self.

"Hi," she smiled. She was wearing a red silk robe, and little red heels with fur around the toes. You could see her baby bump, but because she carried small, she still looked sexy.

"Hi Natalia," I replied as I admired her beauty.

"Come in," she grinned. Her teeth were so white and perfect. Her long brown hair was straightened, and styled like Aaliyah's, and her honey complexion looked supple.

"I brought some non-alcoholic champagne," I lifted it up.

"Well thank you. Follow me," she winked and switched off.

"Where is everybody?" I quizzed.

"Julius is working as usual. I've become so tired of him. Winnie and the kids are gone for a walk, and my mother, she umm, she has passed on," she responded as we walked up the staircase.

"I'm sorry to hear about Ms. Dalia," I said somberly. I was really hoping she made it.

Natalia didn't respond, and continued to lead me to the guest room. I guess she didn't want to do it in she and Julius' room to be safe. We walked into the room, and there were candles lit all around. It smelled like vanilla, and I was getting more and more in the mood. The bed had all black sheets though, which I thought was odd because it took away from the romance.

"Sit down River. Relax," Natalia said seductively. "I'm gonna go change," she bit her lip and then went into the bathroom within the room.

I made myself comfortable on the bed, and squealed excitedly. I couldn't wait to make love to her like I had always dreamed about. I was so tired of masturbating to the videos I'd recorded of her. Plus, now that I was fired, I had run out of new video footage.

The bathroom door creaked, and I knew that meant Natalia was emerging. I turned to look, and there stood Julius. He was wearing a white t-shirt, gray sweats, socks, and eating a candy bar with a gloved hand.

"W-where is Natalia?" I inquired as I shot up off the bed.

"You don't worry about where the fuck she is," he spat as he trashed the candy bar paper. "Sit yo' ass down," he barked when I tried to run and get my gun out of my purse. I was scared as hell.

"You don't deserve her! All those nights you left her here to go to Indiana!" I shouted.

"Don't stick your nose where it doesn't belong. Or better yet, don't stick your tongue where it doesn't belong."

"Natalia!" I called for her as Julius neared me. I felt my bowels loosen, and I knew that I might shit myself any minute now.

"Now my wife asked you politely to leave her alone, but you refused. Correct?" he raised a brow as he towered over me.

His cologne smelled really good, and the candlelight highlighted his gorgeous peanut butter complexion and perfect features. His long eyelashes were like fans, and his full lips made my mouth water. *Maybe I should've tried to sleep with them both*, I thought.

"Yes, but I changed my mind. I will leave her alone, if you let me have one time with you," I smirked. He smirked back, and I knew I had him.

He leaned me back, and we scooted to the middle of the bed. I spread my legs to welcome him, and he ran his finger from my face to my neck. I opened my eyes, and I could see Natalia standing in the doorway. She looked upside down because of the position I was in. I shut my eyes, and felt Julius' fingers part my lips open.

"Oooh," I moaned simply off the thought of him penetrating me.

My mouth stayed ajar, anticipating his next touch. Suddenly, I felt the barrel of a gun slip into my mouth, and before I could protest...

PHEW!

FOUR MONTHS LATER

Life was good now. I had a beautiful family, more money than I could count, and multiple flourishing businesses. All my enemies were gone, and there weren't any hoes waiting in the trenches to break up my relationship. As for Sonia, her hoe ass started fucking with Luke heavily. She wasn't his wifey or anything, but all she needed was a couple bands from him to be happy anyway. That bitch didn't even flinch when she found out Braxton was dead though. As for Leah, she'd kept her promise so far, and hadn't brought her ass back to America. My ears out in Peru said they hadn't seen anything suspicious with her, and that she wasn't making any noise over there either. For the first time in a long time, things were finally looking up.

I turned on Miguel's CD, and let it play softly through the speakers in our bedroom. I had some candles lit, and changed the bedding to all white for the occasion. I spread red and white roses all over the comforter, and all over the floor.

Tonight Natalia and I would end our drought since our new son Julius Christian Tate Jr. was here. We decided to name him after me, because unlike with Jackson, I had become someone that I would want my son to be named after.

I went down to the den to get my wife, and led her up the stairs to our room. I covered her eyes, until we finally got in.

"Oh my gosh Julius," she said in a low tone as she looked around.

"It's time to relax babe," I replied. We'd spent all day with the kids and we were exhausted. However, I was still determined to do this for her.

I led her to the bed, and we both laid down on top of all the rose petals. I grabbed the champagne from the bucket of ice, and poured some into the flutes. I handed one of them to her, and then just looked at her beautiful face.

"What?" she chuckled.

"I have some news for you," I said.

"News?" she raised a brow.

"Yeah, I've decided to let Indiana be run by two of my guys so that I won't have to visit as often," I smiled.

"As often? So how often would you be going now?" she inquired.

"Like twice every six months," I replied and she cheesed. "That's not so bad right?" I ran my finger down her now flat stomach.

"Not at all. I love you Julius," she whispered as she rubbed my face.

"Did you ever think we would come this far?" I chuckled.

"Sometimes I did and other times I didn't, but I'm not surprised at all," she responded.

"You better not be surprised," I said pulling her close to me. "You knew I was never gonna let you go," I bit my lip as I looked down into her eyes.

It was crazy that the teenager I'd met in CVS one random night had become the love of my life. She turned me into a whole new nigga and it was mind blowing. Love and fidelity were two words I knew nothing about unless it dealt with money, until Natalia and my kids came along. I didn't know it was possible to care about someone more than myself, until them.

"I was never gonna leave you," she caressed my face. "Even when I should've," she added.

"I'm glad you didn't," I pecked her lips and began to unbuckle her jean shorts.

I was horny as fuck and couldn't wait to fuck her how I wanted to. The baby was out, and her healing period was over so I could do all kinds of shit. I yanked her shorts and panties down, and she tipped her glass of champagne up.

"Julius, what about the strawberries?" she giggled as she grabbed one and dipped it into whipped cream.

She bit into it as I dipped my head between her smooth thighs. I licked between the slit, and chills went down my spine because of the sweet taste.

"Mmmm," she hummed as she took another bite of the fruit.

I sucked on her clit gently, while gripping her ass cheeks. I pushed my face into her pussy, forcing her to spread her legs even wider.

"Juuu," she whimpered as she balled the comforter into her fists.

Her body jerked lightly as she released into my mouth. I pushed her legs back, and devoured her some more. She was sopping wet, and I licked up all her juices. I ran my hands up her body, and tugged down her tube top once I felt her cum hard in my mouth. I trailed kisses up her sexy body, and pulled her nipple into my mouth. Her small hands caressed the nape of my neck, as I switched back and forth between nipples. I lifted my head and tongued her down, while rubbing between her legs.

"Shit Ju," she cooed in between kisses.

She lightly pushed me on my back, and then planted kisses on my abs. She massaged my balls as she took the tip of my dick into her mouth. She bobbed at a medium pace, while slurping and sucking.

"Damn Nat," I whispered as I palmed the back of her head.

She coated my dick with her saliva, as she made love to it. She was always a beast with her head game. I felt my nut rising when she licked my balls and jacked me off with her spit. She took my dick back into her mouth, and went right back to work.

"Uggghhh," I grunted loudly as I busted in her mouth. A shock wave went through my body, and my damn toes curled.

She swallowed it up, and then mounted her sexy ass above my dick. She sat on the tip, and winced in pain. After pausing for a little bit, she pushed herself down onto my rod. She was so damn tight, and her pussy was drenched. We hadn't had sex in weeks, so we were both savoring this moment here. She bounced up and down slowly, while rocking her hips as well.

"I'm about cum already Ju," she moaned as she stared down into my eyes.

I smacked her ass, and then grabbed it roughly. I watched her small, round, plump titties bounce up and down. She squeezed them as she rode my dick, and I knew I needed to relax before I busted.

"Sexy ass Natalia," I commented and she smirked. She bounced a little faster, and soon enough, she was creaming all over my pole.

I put her on all fours, and pressed her head down into the pillow. I spread her legs wider, and slid myself into her from behind. I spread her ass cheeks so that I could see myself penetrating her tight walls.

"Ahhh, ahhh," she whimpered as I plowed into her.

Her small, round, fat, ass jiggled and bounced, making my dick become harder. I played with her clit, while pumping her in a circular motion.

"Juu, you- uhhh," she called out and then bit the pillow.

"Cum for me," I demanded, and on cue she exploded.

I gripped her waist tightly, and then plowed into her faster and faster. All you could hear was our skin smacking, and my dick slipping in and out of her soaking wet center.

"Arrgghhh," I came so hard, I thought I was gonna black out.

We collapsed on one another, and I craned my neck around to kiss her passionately.

"I love you, daddy," she cooed.

"I love you more baby girl," I replied in between tonguing her down.

"Mommy, I wanna open my gifts now," Jackson whined. It was his fifth birthday, and he was so excited.

"Okay baby, go sit down I'm almost finished," I smiled and rubbed his head.

"Okay," he dropped his head and left the kitchen.

"He looks just like Julius," Winnie chuckled as she helped put the cupcakes onto the tray.

"Yes he does. And he's right, let's get this started so I can eat," Lucy huffed. She was pregnant with her and Rashad's second child together; it was her third. They'd just had a boy named Rashad Jr. a year and a half ago, and got married soon after.

"Grab the number five candle and come on," I shook my head at her. "Julius!" I yelled through the house so he and his friends could come from the den.

I set the tray of cupcakes in front of Jackson, and gave Harmony a look telling her not to touch them yet.

"I'm not, I'm not," she replied smiling and I kissed her cheek.

"The big five!" Julius laughed as he, Rashad, Dash, and Leese entered the kitchen.

"Alright, let's sing!" Winnie shouted as she lit the candle. I picked up my two-year-old, Julius Jr., and then we all started to sing.

We sang happy birthday, then passed out the assorted flavored cupcakes that I'd baked. Once everyone had a cupcake, we let Jackson open his gifts since he was bugging.

"We need to eat before you play," I told him once he was done.

"Yes mommy," he cheesed with his cute self.

Everyone sat down at the dinner table to eat. I smiled as I looked around at everyone, because we had all come so far. I now had three Harmony Bake Shoppe locations, Julius' Club Rissani was still a hit, and we opened two more Jackson Beach Winery's. We were very well off, and we made sure to keep a hefty savings account for rainy days. Julius was still the king of Charleston, Orangeburg, and Indiana, but he traveled very rarely like he had promised. The movie theatres he invested in some years back were flourishing as well.

Lucy owned her own beauty salon, and it was right down the street from the bakery that I worked in. We always went to lunch together, or would go shopping sometimes. There was a time when I thought I'd lost Lucy for good, but we overcame it all.

Six years ago when I was just that sixteen-year-old working at CVS, I never imagined that I would become a happily married mother of three, who owned a successful business. I always thought I would be working in a clothing store until I was fifty-five. Julius was a blessing, although one in disguise, he was one no doubt. I loved him so much, and I was glad that I stuck by his side. God brought us together because we needed each other. Neither one of us knew what it felt like to be loved, but that was something we provided to one another. It was a rocky start, but we had finally come to a smooth road. Nothing could break us up, and nothing could ever come between us.

I looked over at him, as he shared his food with our youngest Julius Jr. I smiled as he talked to him and fed him, because this was not the same guy from the hood back in Indianapolis.

"I love you, honey," I whispered to him as Harmony talked to the table about nonsense, making everyone chuckle.

"I love you more," he replied and pecked my lips softly and longingly.

FIN

BECOME A VIP READER!

*To join my mailing list text **SHVONNE** to **66866** and stay up to date! Also, join **Shvonne Latrice Reading Group** on Facebook!*